A KISS IN PAYMENT

A KISS IN PAYMENT

Stella Ross

Chivers Press • G.K. Hall & Co.
Bath, England   Thorndike, Maine USA

CADCC

EB
MH MK IC MH DM ED VWM BK MC
a JT PW BJK

This Large Print edition is published by Chivers Press, England, and by G.K. Hall & Co., USA.

Published in 1998 in the U.K. by arrangement with Robert Hale Ltd.

Published in 1998 in the U.S. by arrangement with Robert Hale Ltd.

U.K Hardcover ISBN 0–7540–3280–9 (Chivers Large Print)
U.K Softcover ISBN 0–7540–3281–7 (Camden Large Print)
U.S. Softcover ISBN 0–7838–0119–X (Nightingale Series Edition)

The text of this Large Print edition is unabridged.
Other aspects of the book may vary from the original edition.

Set in 16 pt. New Times Roman.

Printed in Great Britain on acid-free paper.

British Library Cataloguing in Publication Data available

Library of Congress Cataloging-in-Publication Data

Ross, Stella.
    A kiss in payment / by Stella Ross.
    p.   cm.
    ISBN 0-7838-0119-X (lg. print : sc : alk. paper)
    1. Large type books.   I. Title.
    [PS3568.O84435K57 1998]
    813'.54—dc21   98-5511

CHAPTER ONE

'Nice work, Solomon! You've polished these silver dishes so brilliantly I can see my face in them.'

Stephanie gave the Arab servant full praise for his efforts.

He smiled and cracked one of his jokes.

'That is good. Maybe your face will stay there after you go. It will give me further incentive.'

She gave a short laugh. She was in no mood for humour. The heat had been oppressive all day. It had brought on another of her migraines.

Anis, one of the waitresses, came into the kitchen in time to catch Solomon's words. She glowered. He was showering compliments on the English manageress again, arousing her jealousy.

Stephanie caught sight of her. It reminded her of her reason for being there.

'Anis—I'd like to see you in my office, please!'

She watched the girl closely as she turned. Anis's sulky face showed a mixture of expressions that were hard to define. She had always lacked the cheerfulness of the rest of the servants.

'What have I done wrong this time?' the

1

Arab girl's tone challenged.

Stephanie kept her displeasure from showing.

'I think you already know,' she said quietly. 'But it's better discussed in private. If you come to my office as soon as you've finished clearing Major Dean's table we'll talk about it then.'

She walked away quickly, ignoring the girl's hostile look.

On the way to her office, that adjoined her suite near the reception area, she met Margery Croxley. As assistant manageress she had been at the North African hotel for years. The oppressive heat didn't seem to worry her.

But the middle-aged woman was aware of the effect it had on Stephanie. She gave her a sympathetic glance.

'You look poorly, my dear. Have you got another of your headaches? Why don't you have a rest? I can do the rounds of the guests. They've nearly all had dinner. I'll order yours for you in your suite, if you like.'

Stephanie thanked her wanly, shaking her head.

'No. I don't feel like eating. But I'll take you up on your offer to do the rounds. If I can summon up the energy I'll take a walk along the cliff when the sun starts to go down. A spot of breeze might make me feel better.'

The other woman nodded. 'Yes—do that. It's always cooler by the sea.'

She followed the younger woman with her

2

eyes as she turned the bend in the corridor, giving a small shrug. If she knew the signs the girl wouldn't be with them long. As it was, she'd only been with them for three months. But the heat got to everyone who was new out from England. Being blonde, the new manageress would probably feel it even more. She was too fair-skinned for this climate.

Stephanie sank into a chair behind her desk. Her head was pounding. For a while she closed her eyes, blocking out the sunlit view from the window. The scenery no longer interested her.

When she had first arrived the colourful gardens had filled her with pleasure. They stretched all the way to the cliffs that bordered the blue Mediterranean. Now, all she longed for was the sight of an English autumn—even rain, drizzle or mist.

Depression filled her. She found herself going over in her mind the circumstances that had brought her there. Was it only six months ago she'd been living happily in Berkshire?

She frowned, reliving her father's tragic accident and all that had followed.

After the estate had been sold she had gone to London to stay with her aunt. It had been vital that she found some sort of job. Constance Reed, who was only ten years her senior, had persuaded Chris Denning to let her become a hostess in his sophisticated night club.

It was not the sort of job Stephanie would have chosen for herself. But there was little else going. And Constance had been manageress there for years.

Within a few weeks of her starting the job, it had been discovered that she was brighter than the rest of his goodlooking hostesses; she had a natural aptitude for administrative work. In order to forget her loss she had thrown herself with relentless energy into her duties, taking over much of her aunt's work when the club was closed during the day.

It had come to Chris's notice. One day he had asked her to his office. It was plushly furnished and had a two way mirror system so that he could oversee the bar and restaurant below whenever he chose without being observed.

She had sat there feeling slightly embarrassed. Chris's reputation was well-known. She had been warned by some of his other hostesses that one day he would probably make a pass at her. Rumours of his many affairs were rife amongst his staff.

It had come as a shock when, with his first words, he had offered her promotion.

'How would you like to take over the managership of my hotel at Maris el Akben?'

She had gasped. 'Why me?'

He'd fixed her with his lazy, grey eyes, giving a laugh.

'Why not? My father believed in backing hunches. He gave your aunt the managership of The Sunflower Club when she was only twenty-four. You're twenty-five—extremely attractive—and intelligent. Both of those last attributes are important.'

She had dropped her gaze, flattered by his trust more than his compliments. She was not one of those who'd fallen for his charms immediately like a lot of the other women he employed.

From what she had heard, he was a playboy like his father. It was common knowledge that Sir Geoffrey Denning had once had an affair with her aunt, and it had caused her divorce.

'Don't answer immediately,' Chris had told her. 'Think it over. But don't take too long. I'm flying out there next week. If you accept I'll take you with me.'

She had discussed it with her aunt. Constance had encouraged her.

'Snap it up. It'll be a good change for you. You mustn't allow yourself to brood over the past. Your father's accident will take time to forget. I loved him, too. He was my brother. If I was you, I'd get right out of the country. Take the post Chris has very generously offered you.'

Stephanie had taken a few more days to consider, and then she had seen her employer and accepted.

He'd smiled. 'I think you're a difficult person to please. If I'd offered the job to any of the other girls downstairs they'd have jumped at it. Why did you take so long?'

She avoided his eyes. They had a hypnotic

5

effect on her.

'I like to be certain before I rush into trouble,' she said quietly. 'Anyway—you told me to think it over.'

'That's true.' He'd brought their interview to an end quickly. 'Well—take the rest of the week off. You'll need time to make arrangements. I'll let Constance know the time and place of our departure.'

*   *   *

Chris had used his own private plane, piloting it himself. She had even found herself growing mildly excited as they'd taken off, flying towards the land of sunshine.

He had stayed at the North African hotel for a few days to see her safely settled in, giving her advice and tips on dealing with foreign servants. She had even found herself relaxing in his company. But, in the back of her mind, she was fully aware of the danger of falling for his charms. He was only a few years older than her and fatally attractive. However, not once had he taken advantage of their closeness.

After he'd returned to England she had pushed his existence away. Her work in the hotel was exacting.

Later, as the summer had grown hotter, she'd begun to suffer from migraine. Sometimes the tropical heat had nearly driven her mad.

She felt ill now. For a brief moment she wondered whether her discomfort could possibly have any bearing on her attitude towards Anis. Maybe she was being unduly critical of the Arab girl.

She shook her head, discounting it at once. The girl had been abominably rude to one of the guests. She needed a stern 'telling off'.

Major Dean had merely asked for a change of linen. He had inadvertently spilt some wine. It would have attracted flies if it had been left.

The girl had changed it with bad grace. She had even dared to answer him back, telling him they were short of table cloths. The man had tried to laugh off her rudeness.

Stephanie had observed the incident from a short distance away. It was too bad that the mild, good-humoured man should have been put through such a humiliating scene.

When Anis's knock sounded on the door she called out 'Come in' more sharply than she might otherwise have done.

The Arab girl came sullenly into the room.

Stephanie left her to stand while she replaced some papers in a drawer. As she looked up she thought she caught a look of malicious hatred in the other girl's eyes.

For a moment it threw her. She found herself faltering. Then she tossed the feeling away as imagination.

'Anis—you know why you're here. We can't have such behaviour in the hotel. I observed you being rude to a guest. If Mr Denning were to hear about it you'd receive instant dismissal. He'll overlook a lot of things—but not rudeness. You understand what I'm saying to you?'

The girl gave her a sly look.

'That would make you happy then, wouldn't it?'

Stephanie felt her eyes widen. 'What do you mean by that?'

Anis grew hysterical.

'You know very well, Miss Hartland! You have stolen the affections of the man I love. And now you wish to send me away so that I will not make bother for you . . .'

Stephanie felt her head spin. The girl wasn't making sense. She passed a hand over her clammy brow. Perhaps the heat had finally succeeded in driving her insane.

The girl's tirade was continuing.

'Don't pretend you treat Solomon the same way as you treat the rest of us. It is clear you're attracted to him. You laugh together. You behave with him as you would a man of your own race. It is of no concern to you that Solomon and I are betrothed. You try to snatch him from me . . .'

The girl's meaning became clear. But Stephanie found the accusation totally ludicrous.

'Be quiet!' She heard herself snapping. 'Do you want everyone in the hotel to hear your ridiculous rambling? Go back to your work! If I hear of you being rude to anyone else you can pack your things immediately.'

The girl ran from the room, slamming the door behind her.

Stephanie stared hard at the wall. Then she closed her eyes, tears of pain and self-pity starting to well.

Why—oh, why had she ever agreed to come to this steamy, hell-hot country where servants went berserk and the sun never seemed to stop shining?

She put her head in her hands. Her migraine was worse than ever. She longed to lie down in the cool. But, even in her comfortable, air conditioned suite the atmosphere was too oppressive.

She breathed a determined sigh. Tomorrow she would write to Chris and tell him she'd had enough. He would have to send a replacement for her as soon as possible.

But now, her immediate need was for a breath of air.

She headed out of her office, through the reception area and into the garden. Close to the cliff she saw the breeze moving in a tall clump of eucalyptus trees that marked the start of the coastal path. She walked slowly towards them.

Sitting on a bench beneath their shade, she gathered the strength to go on.

The coastal path was well-known to the staff

9

and visitors of the Moorish hotel. It was a local beauty spot, providing spectacle.

Stephanie set off, taking the lower route when she came to the fork along the path. It was here where it descended through the pines and ran sometimes within inches of the cliff edge.

A breeze from the sea began to lift her hair from her hot forehead. Slowly her headache started to ease. It left room for her to think again about Anis's ridiculous statement. She began to find it mildly disconcerting.

Had she unwittingly given anyone else the impression that she was interested in Solomon? It would have been awful if she had.

She remembered the conversations she'd had with Chris. Before he'd left for England he'd given her strict instructions on how to treat the Arab staff. Familiarity made them lazy and contemptuous of taking orders. Over-friendliness was not to be encouraged.

Acting on her own judgement, she had tried to strike a happy medium, treating them with civility and courtesy—giving praise when it was truly deserved.

Had she gone too far with Solomon?

She had always found him one of the easiest servants to get on with. He was a student they were employing temporarily. His home was in the near by town. But, like the others, he slept at the hotel.

He was about twenty-one, good-looking and

always willing to please. She found his keen sense of humour refreshing. And his English was excellent.

Maybe she had unintentionally favoured him?

She found the thought disturbing, pushing it out of her mind. It was a relief that she'd decided to leave. It would have been unbearable if Anis had started spreading some silly rumour.

She stopped and turned purposefully. It might be as well if she went back and wrote her letter to Chris now, while her head was clear. Tomorrow, when the sun was at its height, her migraine would undoubtedly return.

She began to make her way back in the cool of the sunset.

It was as she did so that she perceived a movement on the lonely path ahead of her. A figure stepped from behind a pine. Stephanie stopped with a small, spiked feeling of apprehension.

CHAPTER TWO

Solomon stood in the centre of the path with the last rays of the setting sun glinting on his sleekly oiled hair.

For a moment Stephanie remained where she was, her apprehension growing. Then she

11

tried to cover it, walking to meet him.

'Hello! What are you doing away from the hotel? Is all the clearing up done?'

He smiled, showing gleaming white teeth.

'Yes, Miss Hartland. It is all finished.'

Embarrassment at meeting him so soon after hearing Anis's accusation made her tear her eyes away from his.

She glanced at her watch. 'Are you sure all the work's done? I wouldn't have thought the dining room was completely empty yet.'

Solomon gave a small laugh.

'You worry too much. And you, yourself, work too hard. I tell you everything is being attended to. Abdullah is completing what little there is left.'

His familiarity left her tonguetied. She was aware of his interested gaze taking in every detail of her form beneath her thin dress.

Her words came out stiltedly.

'But that's really not good enough. Abdullah has enough work of his own. I find it insulting that you should take it upon yourself to dole out your own work to other servants.'

Solomon's reply came back in a tone that was meant to be reassuring.

'I promise you that everything is all right. And I have rewarded Abdullah handsomely. He will not mind staying on so that you and I can be alone together.'

His words appalled her.

'You mean you followed me here?'

He smiled. 'Yes—I followed you. I observe your movements on many occasions. By your kind attitude to me ever since I entered the hotel's employ I did not think you would mind.'

She found her voice shaking.

'Then you were completely wrong. I wish to be on my own. Please let me pass. We'll discuss what you've just said in the morning when you've come to your senses.'

He stood his ground. There was no room for her to get by unless she diverted into the bushes. To have done so would have been unseemly.

She watched a look of reproach come into his expression.

'Why do you say that to me? Is it the way a woman behaves in your country when she has allowed a man to see her interest? If it is you must teach me these customs. I should like to court you and I wish to know how your mind works.'

Panic at his statement rose inside her.

'You've completely misunderstood. I have no interest in you—other than as an employee. Please, Solomon, let me pass!'

Bewilderment filled his dark eyes.

'No—I will not. You are playing some curious game with me. Did you not realise that everything I have done since coming to the hotel has been for love of you? I have even given up my studies to stay on as a mere kitchen boy in order to be near you.'

She shook her head wildly. 'I didn't realise that. I'm terribly sorry. But we can discuss all this when we get back to the hotel.'

She made an attempt to pass. The situation was getting out of hand and she was in a lonely position far away from the safety of the hotel.

As she stepped clumsily into the trees he took her arm angrily.

'I think this is better discussed here and now.'

She looked down at his dark hand.

'Please let me go!' she cried firmly.

He refused, challenging her eyes with his own. His voice showed an ominous lack of respect.

'You are convincing me that you have been trifling with my affections. Please stay until you have told me why you have done that.'

She uttered a small cry.

'You're hurting my arm. It's dangerous to quarrel on this path. One of us might fall in the sea.'

His eyes upbraided her.

'Do you think that matters to me? After what you have done death would be a kind thing.'

Her eyes showed her fear of him. He saw it and dragged her roughly into his embrace, uttering words of Arab endearment as she struggled to escape.

Suddenly he broke into English.

'I love you! I want you! You will not break

14

my heart this way.'

She broke free and gave a scream.

He pulled her towards him again and pressed his lips on hers. For a moment she felt herself suffocating, the scent of his oiled hair pervading her nostrils.

When eventually he freed her she felt revolted.

'How dare you?' she breathed. 'You disgust me. When we get back I shall have you fired without notice.'

He stared at her with disbelief.

'You are telling me my love means nothing to you?'

She grew furious.

'Of course it means nothing. I find you repugnant. I shall be leaving the hotel as soon as Mr Denning can find a replacement.'

She turned and fled.

For a moment she fondly believed he would allow her to escape. In order to reach the hotel quicker, she made for the steep slope that separated the lower path from the one above. It halted her progress. Soon she heard Solomon give chase behind.

Panic filled her heart. She had nearly traversed the slope when he grabbed at the hem of her dress bringing her down.

For a moment all the breath was knocked from her body. She lay panting with exertion on the pine covered hill while he brought his face, contorted with fury, menacingly close to hers.

15

'I shall not be returning to the hotel,' he rasped. 'There is nothing there for me now. But first I shall show you that my respect for you had entirely flown. Since you have dishonoured me I shall repay you.'

She gave a scream. It was easy to guess the fate in store for her.

He covered her mouth with one hand, tearing at the bodice of her dress with the other. She heard the material give, and saw the glint of lust light his eyes as the bare flesh of her breasts was exposed.

The next minutes were the longest in her life. Terror stricken she began to feel the grope of his hand.

After a while he removed his hand from her mouth and his lips closed over hers. She was aware of his breath coming in a series of choking sobs. They matched her own. But hers were through fear and not passion.

Mercilessly he reduced her garments to shreds and she prayed for oblivion.

It didn't come. But, as his eagerness increased, she knew there might come one moment when he would have to release her.

When that moment came she was ready for it. Bringing up her legs and lunging at his chest she made one last desperate attempt to get free.

The force she had to use sent him hurtling down the slope.

She didn't wait for the outcome. Sobbing,

she made her way blindly to the path above.

It was dark when she reached the clump of eucalyptus trees. Through them she could see the lights of the hotel and wept with relief.

How she crossed the garden she never knew. Her fear only began to fade after she had reached the Moorish archway at the entrance to the hotel. There, half fainting, she stopped to regain her breath, leaning against its rough architecture.

Shame filled her at all she had been through. It taunted her pride. How could she be seen entering the hotel in the state she was in? She had lost most of her dress and had mislaid a shoe. Her hair was in disarray and covered with twigs.

If she told Margery she would insist on sending for Inspector Abusaid. She would be forced to charge Solomon with attempted rape. It would mean staying in North Africa— reliving the incident time and time again. Her spirit quailed.

She remembered Solomon's words. '... I shall not be returning ...' They gave her the way out she was seeking. If she could enter the hotel without being seen, she would never have to breathe a word to anyone of her disgrace.

*　　　*　　　*

For the next half an hour she waited trembling behind a thick palm that sheltered the doorway. The moment her chance came, she took it, gliding like a ghost to her apartment.

Once there she sank to her knees, weeping fresh tears. The horror of the episode finally overcame her.

Much later she ran a bath, immmersing her body in it. Using more than her usual amount of soap, she scrubbed herself, trying to rid her thoughts of the man who had abused her.

When she had finished, she put what remained of her garments into a bag, placing them in a cupboard out of sight. Tomorrow she would burn everything that might remind her of the episode.

Margery rang her as she was pouring herself a stiff drink. She picked up the receiver with trepidation.

'Ah, you're there,' the assistant manageress said with relief. 'I'm just checking, my dear. I saw you go out but I didn't see you return. How's the headache? You weren't looking at all well when you left.'

Stephanie kept the strain from showing in her voice.

'I'm feeling better,' she replied quietly.

'Oh, that's fine. Your walk must have done you good. Well—I'll see you when we have our usual chat in the morning. There's nothing to report. Everything in the hotel is proceeding on its usual shiny wheels. Have a good sleep, dear . . .'

Stephanie interrupted her.

'I'd like to speak to Chris Denning. Would you dial his number at the Sunflower Club if you're at reception?'

The other woman sounded surprised. 'In London, you mean? Why, yes, of course. Is it anything I can talk to him about to save you the trouble?'

'No,' Stephanie replied. 'It's personal. Good night, Margery.'

When the phone rang again it was Chris. The assistant manageress's voice sounded over the top.

'You're through!'

Stephanie didn't hear her put down the other receiver. But she didn't really care.

Chris's voice sounded anxious.

'Stephanie—is that you?'

'Yes. I want a replacement at once,' she told him.

For a moment he didn't reply. When he did his voice was brusque.

'I'm afraid that's not so easy to arrange. And, much as I like to hear your voice, I think you could have written. What's happened to make you ring at this time of night with such a request?'

She kept her voice even.

'I'm afraid I can't tell you. But the climate's never suited me. I believe I mentioned that before. Anyway—I *must* have a replacement. If you don't promise to send someone I shall leave without notice. Is that clear?'

19

His voice came back angrily.

'I don't care for your attitude. It makes me wonder just who's employing who.'

She found herself pleading with him.

'*You* made me come out here. And I can't take it any longer. You've got to find someone else—please!'

His anger disappeared.

'What's the matter with you, Stephanie? Are you crying?'

She stifled a sob with the back of her hand.

'No—no—I'm all right. But I've got to leave here.'

'Very well. I'll see what I can do. Hopefully, I'll get someone on a plane tomorrow. Will that suit you?'

She broke down.

'Yes—that will do. I'll get packed. I didn't mean to sound intentionally rude. It's very good of you . . .'

She replaced the receiver, giving way to tears once more.

Margery, who had put down the phone in reception at the same time, heard her through the wall of the apartment. The sound of the young woman's distress was upsetting.

She went to knock on her door, but decided against it. If the girl still had her headache she wouldn't thank her for butting in. Anyway— soon she'd be out of it. She'd have another new manager to get used to. She'd always known the young woman was far too fair-skinned for this climate.

CHAPTER THREE

When morning came Stephanie had recovered a lot from her ordeal. She gave the news to Margery about her departure after they had discussed the menus.

'I shall be leaving shortly,' she told her. 'As you know, I rang Mr Denning last night. He's promised to send a replacement today.'

The older woman feigned surprise.

'Oh, I'm so sorry. But I'm happy for your sake,' she went on kindly. 'I know you've never really settled in here. Quite honestly, I'm surprised you've stuck it as long as you have. The heat's been oppressive—even for me. And you've complained of headaches for the last couple of months.'

Stephanie frowned. 'I hope I haven't made myself a bore.'

The assistant manageress laughed.

'I shouldn't have put it that way. What I meant was you've suffered.' She stopped and her laugh faded. 'But I shall miss you. I sincerely mean that. It's been nice having another English woman on the staff. I expect we shall go back to men now.'

Stephanie looked down at her desk.

'Yes—well—I'm sorry.'

21

A wall of silence came between them. Although Stephanie had always found the older woman helpful and sympathetic they had never really been friends. Margery was inclined to be gossipy. It came out strongly in her change of subject.

'Oh, by the way—we've lost our kitchen boy. You know—Solomon—the one who seemed to take quite a fancy to you. I'm afraid he scarpered last night without even taking his things. It's a bit inconvenient. We'll have to get one of the others to take over his work until we can find someone else. But that won't be too difficult.'

She stopped and mused.

'It's not unusual for servants to skip off without notice. We've had it often before. But, I must say, I'm surprised he didn't smuggle his things out—plus half the kitchen silver. Anis, his girl friend, is throwing a bit of a tantrum. Evidently he didn't tell her of his intentions . . .'

Stephanie got up quickly, scraping back her chair on the tiled floor. She went over to the window, hiding her expression.

'Please, Margery, I'd rather not have this to deal with. I had a brush with Anis yesterday—as you may or may not know. And I'd prefer you didn't use that expression again—about Solomon fancying me. I find it rather revolting.'

Margery studied the other's slim back.

'I'm dreadfully sorry. I didn't mean it to sound offensive. I thought you might even have taken it as a compliment. He was an educated person—not the usual trash. Far too good for that silly Anis, if you ask me . . .'

'Please—' Stephanie put a hand to her forehead. She fought to keep her voice under control as she turned.

'Look—if we've discussed everything, I think I'll start packing. I've brought everything up to date. My replacement will find all the books in order.'

Margery looked at her curiously.

'I'm sorry. I can tell your migraine's coming back. I'm afraid it's going to be hot again.' She stood up. 'Right—well—I'll sort out Anis. If she gets too stroppy I'll send her packing. She's been treading on a lot of people's toes lately. I think she's getting too big for her boots . . .'

Stephanie waited for the door to close. Then she went straight to her apartment, taking the bag of clothes she had worn the previous night out of the cupboard. Without anyone seeing, she took them to the incinerator.

*   *   *

The rest of the morning passed smoothly. Stephanie stayed in her suite, focussing all her attention on her packing. With luck she would be leaving later in the day. If necessary she would stay in Tunis until a return flight became

23

available.

She found her one shoe. She had left it in the bathroom the night before. It should have been taken to the incinerator with the rest of her clothes. But it was too late now. There would be too many inquisitive people around.

She tucked it into the wastepaper basket in her adjoining office.

At lunchtime, she was disturbed to find that the waitress who brought her meal to her suite was none other than Anis.

Her unease gathered as she noticed the girl's tear-stained face. She prayed she would leave without another scene. But it was in vain.

The girl put the tray on the table before facing Stephanie with blazing eyes.

'This is all your doing!'

Stephanie hid her expression.

'What do you mean by that?'

The Arab girl's fury came out. 'Something you have said or done has made Solomon leave. You need not deny that because I know it for certain.'

Stephanie regarded the other girl in silence.

Anis went on. 'Solomon followed you after you left the hotel last evening. I saw you both from the place where I was on the terrace. First, I saw you go—walking through the pines towards the sea. Then, later, I saw Solomon.' She went on boldly, 'You can't say that is untrue because I see it all in your face. You made an arrangement to meet him, didn't you?

24

You sent him a note . . .'

Stephanie didn't reply. She saw the other girl's eyes narrow menacingly.

'What did you say to him?' she demanded. 'And what did you do—there together in the pines?'

Stephanie's silence acted as a goad to Anis. She began to cry hysterically.

'I have heard you are leaving. Why is that? Are you going away together? Is it all lies about you returning to England?'

When Stephanie's reply eventually came it wasn't harsh. She even found it in her heart to pity the Arab girl. Solomon had treated her with utter indifference.

'You're wrong, Anis,' she heard herself saying. 'There are things I can't tell you. But I'm going back to England alone. I think you're probably well rid of Solomon. One day you'll forget him. You'll meet someone worthy who'll love you in return.'

The girl shook her head wildly.

'Never! I love only Solomon. And you have made him leave. Somehow I shall think of a way to hurt you as you have hurt me.'

She flew from the room, leaving Stephanie to stare shakenly after her.

The Arab girl's threat stayed in her mind for a long time, although Stephanie tried to push it aside. There was nothing the girl could do to harm her, and tomorrow she would be far away from the hotel. She must try to forget about it.

She completed her packing, piling the cases into her office.

Later in the afternoon she heard a commotion coming from the grounds. A girl's high pitched scream, sounding like the wail of a muezzin, sent a cold thrill of foreboding through her.

From her window she saw Anis come tearing through the clump of eucalyptus.

*   *   *

Even before Margery entered her office to tell her the tragic news that Solomon had been found dead at the bottom of the cliff she was half aware of it.

She listened dully to the woman's monologue.

'Naturally, I've given the poor girl some aspirin. It must have come as a terrible shock. I can't *think* what I'd have done if I'd suddenly come across a dead body. *And* the body of someone she'd loved. That must have been even worse.

'Of course, it will mean a lot of rather nasty publicity for the hotel. The police will want to know all the "ins and outs". We'll probably be inundated by Inspector Abusaid and his men very shortly.

'They'll want to know why the poor boy should have wanted to take his life. And, of course, it could only have been suicide. There's no one in the hotel who could possibly have wanted to murder the lad. He was always so friendly and easy to get on with.'

She brushed a hand across her forehead.

'I must say, I rather envy you getting out of all this just in time. I don't know what your replacement will think when they come out today. I wouldn't be surprised if they catch the first plane back. We've been rather unlucky with our managers lately . . .'

*   *   *

Stephanie refused her dinner when it was brought to her that evening. Ever since she had heard the news of Solomon's death she had searched her heart, wondering how his death had occurred.

Had she inadvertently caused it when she had lunged out at him in order to escape? Or had he thrown himself over when he'd come to his senses, filled with remorse for what he'd tried to do?

In spite of her hatred for him her conscience refused to give her any peace.

Early in the evening a knock sounded on her office door. She expected it to be her replacement. A plane had been due to land at the nearby airport a half an hour earlier. She had sent a car to meet it.

Her expectation died when she found her caller was the local Inspector of police. Beside

27

him was his sergeant. Both were in uniform.

Her heart dropped.

The educated Arab smiled politely. 'Good evening, Miss Hartland. Such a tragic thing to have occurred at the hotel while you are managing it. You have my heartfelt sympathy.'

She gave a nod of thanks. They had met on one occasion before. He had seemed friendly.

'I wonder—' he went on kindly—'if you would mind giving me some answers to some questions? If it would not be putting you to too much trouble, might my man and I be permitted to come in?'

Her hand shook as she opened the door wider.

'Of course,' she muttered.

Inspector Abusaid showed her a flash of white teeth. As the sergeant closed the door behind them she felt her awkwardness grow.

What kind of questions would he ask?

He chose a comfortable chair after she had seated herself behind her desk, leaving his sergeant to stand.

'I do hope it is permissable for me to sit while we chat. This heat is exhausting, is it not? I have been walking on the cliff. I find exercise in this extreme heat very tiring.'

'Would you like me to order you a cool drink?' she asked.

'Ah—no—no—that is quite unnecessary.' He glanced at the cases stacked against the wall before going on. 'Oh, someone is going away?'

28

She nodded tightly.

He went on. 'Surely not you? I believe you have only been in Maris el Akben for three months? Is that not right?'

She found his tone searching. She fought to keep her voice under control.

'Yes, that's right. But the heat upsets me. It's been making me ill. I hope to leave first thing in the morning. I'm waiting for my replacement to arrive.'

Inspector Abusaid's face took on a disappointed look.

'Ah—that is a great pity. Sadly, we have only met on one other occasion. That was that rather trivial affair of pilfering here, if you remember. Curiously, I had made a note that I should invite you to my house on a suitable social occasion.' He shrugged his shoulders. 'But, unfortunately, I am kept rather busy. We have a constant variety of petty crime in our little town, as I expect your English policemen have, also.'

She agreed. It had occurred to her that the man was merely making polite conversation in order to put her at her ease.

Did he already know about her meeting with Solomon on the cliff? Were these just preliminaries to asking further, deeper questions?

She waited.

The man didn't beat about the bush any longer. 'This unfortunate man, Solomon

Feroud,' he began. 'Since he was in your employ I wonder if you can possibly tell me anything you know that might have some bearing on his death?'

She struggled with her conscience, taking a deep breath before replying.

'No. I know of nothing,' she said sharply. 'I'm sorry he's dead. He was a good employee.'

The man examined her with a searching look. She felt her colour rise.

With a jerky movement she rose to her feet, hoping to bring their interview to an end.

'Well, if that's all you wanted to know, I wonder if you'd forgive me now? I have several more things to do before I leave. I haven't entirely finished my packing.'

When Inspector Abusaid made no attempt to rise her heart sank.

Instead, he put up a well manicured hand thoughtfully to his cheek.

'Yes, of course, you are going away. Perhaps you would tell something about your decision to leave. It was all rather sudden, wasn't it? Miss Croxley tells me that you only told her this morning.'

She knew he had only been playing with her earlier. He knew all about her intention to leave.

She felt herself colouring. 'Yes, that's correct. But I made the decision long before that. I told you—the heat was making me ill.'

'And so you wrote to Mr Denning and asked

him to send a replacement?'

She faltered. If she told another lie it could easily be traced back.

'No,' she said quietly. 'I rang him last evening.'

He smiled at her. 'Yes, that's right. Miss Croxley inadvertently listened in. I think it was good that you told me the truth.'

She gave a gasp. The man's tone had hardened. As he studied her his eyes were dark and cold.

'And now, Miss Hartland, perhaps we can stop this game of pretence. I would like you to sit down and consider my previous question. If you like, I can repeat it. Would you please tell me if you know of anything that can have any bearing on Solomon Feroud's death? I must tell you that a member of your staff saw you heading in the same direction, but separately, last evening. I am suggesting that you met the unfortunate young man on the cliff. A shoe was found there. It is of English make. It is of the size that I think would fit a lady of your stature . . .'

He saw her eyes drop to the nearby wastepaper basket. Following her gaze he caught sight of the red strap of a half hidden shoe. With a satisfied sigh he bent briefly and picked it out.

Holding it up, his eyes showed a gleam of triumph.

'Ah, here is its partner.' He remained silent,

31

savouring his power over her. 'And now, Miss Hartland, I would strongly advise you to tell me the truth of that meeting. My sergeant here is a fast shorthand writer. He will take down everything you say. But, if you wish, you may contact a lawyer before so doing . . .'

Stephanie's eyes grew wide.

'I've no need of a lawyer. I've done nothing wrong . . .'

She caught sight of the inspector's accusing look. It filled her with dread. Sinking into her chair, she bowed her head.

'Very well—I *did* lie to you. I'm extremely sorry. But my meeting with Solomon had nothing to do with his death.' Her voice shook. 'I met him by accident when I was returning from my walk. He'd followed me . . .' She hesitated.

'Please go on,' he prompted.

She gave a sob, continuing tearfully. 'He tried to rape me. I fought him off and fled back to the hotel. My clothes were torn. I waited outside the hotel until I could go in unseen. Then I bathed and rang Mr Denning. I begged him to send a replacement.'

'You gave him the reason, of course.'

'No.' She shook her head fiercely. 'It was something I never wanted to tell anyone. I just begged him to send a replacement. I told him I would leave without one if he didn't.'

The inspector studied her bent head. He gave a sigh.

'I see. And you have your torn clothes, of course?'

She looked up at him.

'No. I burnt them this morning in the incinerator. I wanted nothing to remind me of what had happened.'

He was briefly silent before saying, 'Then, presumably, if you struggled against rape you will have many bruises. I imagine that you will not mind being examined by my doctor?'

She gave him a look of astonishment.

'You can't possibly be doubting what I've told you?'

His cold look told her nothing.

'I merely require substantiating evidence. If you are bringing a charge of attempted rape against the dead man then I need proof.'

Her voice rose. 'But Solomon's dead! He can't answer that charge. And I don't want to bring one.' She became hysterical. 'I just want to leave North Africa and forget about it. You can't realise the terror I went through . . .'

He interrupted her harshly.

'My dear Miss Hartland, your actions on returning to the hotel were hardly those of one terrorised. First, you wait rationally and perceptively outside this busy hotel until you can escape to your suite unseen. Then you bathe. After that you ring Mr Denning to ask for a replacement without giving him the reason. Then, this morning, you burn your torn clothes.' His eyes narrowed. 'Those are the actions of someone who has something deeper to hide.'

She found herself floundering. 'But I've told you. I didn't want anyone to know. I felt so ashamed.'

He shook his head with disbelief.

'If what you have told me is the truth, then there is no shame attached to you—only to the man.' His tone became furtive. 'Unless, of course, you in some way brought the attack upon yourself. Perhaps even aggravated it. It is not so unusual for some women to be—what is the English term?—turned on by sexual violence.'

She stared at him, feeling the colour drain from her face.

'How dare you!' She rose to her feet, struggling to escape an overwhelming sense of faintness. 'How dare you suggest such a vile thing!'

The door opened abruptly as she was fighting a losing battle against a wall of dark mist.

Chris Denning was standing in the doorway. He saw her plight at once and dashed to help her.

'Thank God!' she breathed. 'Oh, thank God you've come!'

Like a stone, she collapsed into his arms.

CHAPTER FOUR

When Stephanie recovered she found herself lying on her bed in her apartment.

Chris, who was standing by the window with his back to her, heard her moan and turned abruptly.

'How are you?' he asked, coming over to her. 'You've been out for about half an hour. I was getting worried.'

She made an attempt to sit up but he restrained her.

'I shouldn't do that. Just lie quietly for a while. Would you like a drink—or some tea? Perhaps a couple of aspirin?'

She shook her head, memory of the recent ordeal with Inspector Abusaid returning. Tears filled her eyes.

'I want to go home. I just want to go home.'

Chris studied her.

She looked back at him in a dazed way. 'How did you get here? I thought you were going to send a replacement—not come yourself.'

He gave a shrug. 'It was impossible to find a replacement for you at such short notice. It left me no option. Anyway, you sounded very unlike your normal self on the phone. I was a little concerned.'

She dragged her eyes away. 'The whole thing's like a nightmare.'

He examined her again, his manner altering. 'From what I've been told you have only yourself to blame. You damned little idiot! What did I tell you about getting too friendly with the servants? Didn't you think something like this might happen?'

She flinched. 'Please don't shout at me. That remark's completely uncalled for!'

'Oh, really—?' He put his hand into his pocket, taking out a piece of typed paper. 'Then maybe you'd care to hear this. It's a copy of part of Anis's statement. It makes very choice reading. Inspector Abusaid, who happens to be an old friend of mine, let me read it. He thought I might be interested—since I'm likely to be standing bail for you to the tune of several thousand pounds.'

She gasped as he began to read out loud.

'—"*Miss Hartland and Solomon used to check the stores together. It was obvious they were having an affair. I used to hear them always joking and laughing. One night when I was going to bed I heard Miss Hartland's voice coming from Solomon's room. I heard her whisper to him. Her words were quite clear.*

'*She said*—"*Our affair must stop. It is not fitting that I should let you make love to me like this. I am English. You are only an Arab servant. Our relationship must end. It has been amusing. Now it is all over*" ...'

'Stop! It's not true,' Stephanie wept. 'How can anyone possibly believe that pack of lies? The girl is jealous. She hates me. She promised to find some way of hurting me.'

36

Chris showed no sign of relenting. He went on sarcastically.

'This Solomon—you really went for him, eh? You gave him preferential treatment, and then ended up having an affair with him. After that you regretted it. You tried to end it but he wasn't having any. So you lured him along that lonely cliff. Then you pushed him to his death and ripped your clothes to make it look as though you'd been attacked . . .'

She broke down completely.

'It's not true—it's not true! I never encouraged Solomon in that way. I only gave him praise when it was deserved. But he misunderstood. He followed me—and then he attacked and tried to rape me. I never wanted anyone to know the shame of what I'd been through . . .'

She sobbed like a child into her pillow.

Chris stood looking down at her for a moment. Then his manner altered again. He put a comforting hand on her shoulder.

'OK! It's all right, Stephanie.'

She shook his hand away, continuing to weep hysterically.

His voice grew harsh again. 'Now—stop that! I believe you. But it was necessary to get your reaction. It stands out a mile the statement's a lie. But I had to be completely sure. I don't care to risk losing a lot of money over a girl who might run out on her bail.'

She stared back at him with disbelief.

'You really thought I was that kind of person!'

He dropped his eyes.

'I'm a business man—not a philanthropist.'

She sobbed into her pillow once more.

He stood up and moved towards the door.

'Well, I should get some more rest, if I were you. You're going to need a lot of strength and a lot of courage. We're not out of the wood yet.'

She sat up before he left.

'What will they do?' she asked tormentedly.

He looked back at her. It was no use raising her hopes.

'The inspector will probably be back within the hour. I should think he'll either charge you with murder—or manslaughter.'

He watched her blue eyes open wide. Pity overcame him.

'Naturally, I'll arrange the best lawyer possible. And I'll stand your bail. I don't think Abusaid will have any objection. My main concern at the moment is keeping you out of their filthy jail.'

'But I haven't done anything!' she cried.

It unleashed his anger.

'You should have stuck more firmly to my instructions. I warned you not to get friendly with the staff but you flouted my warning. I won't allow any of my staff to think they know better than me . . .'

He stopped suddenly. The girl's look was wearing him down. He hated his weakness in

38

being so attracted to her. She deserved his wrath because of all the trouble she was putting him to. It sparked him to frighten her more.

'But I shouldn't let the thought of a trial worry you. Just practise the injured little woman act. It always goes down well with a jury!'

He slammed the door, leaving her to stare after him.

*   *   *

During the next few days Stephanie's life became even more of a nightmare. The police visited her several times and she was taken to the local station.

Chris accompanied her. As he had anticipated, she was charged with the lesser crime of manslaughter.

He employed a lawyer for her who prevented her from adding anything more to the statement she'd already given.

Later, in her meetings with him, she was made to repeat in detail everything that she could remember about the incident. Through repetition it became firmly locked in her mind. She knew she would never forget it. It would haunt her dreams if she ever gained freedom.

Alone in her suite, occasionally Chris would keep her company. He became a tower of strength. Often Stephanie was tearful and depressed. He tried to rebuild her confidence.

It was impossible to venture out during the day. Newspaper reporters haunted the grounds. Stephanie had become notorious overnight.

One evening he knocked on her door.

'It's dark,' he told her, 'and there's no one around. I made sure of that. I think it would do you good if you had a stroll.'

She drew back instinctively.

'Not on your own,' he said quickly. 'What sort of fool do you take me for?' His tone relaxed. 'I meant with me. Put on a jumper. The air's cool.'

Reluctantly she obeyed. They slipped out together through the hotel's reception area.

Once in the garden they strolled without speaking.

Suddenly Stephanie stopped by a clump of azaleas. Their heavy perfume filled the air. The scent reminded her, with a sickening feeling, of the brilliantine Solomon had used.

Shuddering, she covered her face with her hands.

Chris glanced at her. 'What's the matter?' he asked. 'Are you cold?'

She shook her head. Her words came out despondently.

'I *did* cause his death, you know. He must have fallen over the edge of the cliff when I lunged at him . . .'

He admonished her sharply.

'That's not for you to decide. Forget it!'

She looked back at him wildly.

'But I can't forget it. The lawyer makes me repeat what I remember time after time. I *know* I caused his death. It's quite clear he couldn't have fallen over the cliff any other way. I just didn't want to believe it before.'

She grew hysterical. He shook her by the shoulders roughly.

'Shut up! If you allow yourself to believe that you'll never convince a jury. And what does it matter how he met his death? He attacked you. He didn't deserve to live.'

He let her go and searched her face, thinking how lovely she was in spite of her woeful expression. For a moment he gave way to what he felt for her.

'You must think all men are made up of brute force and violence. I couldn't imagine you ever wanting anything to do with them any more. Your experience must have sickened you for life. Even me—I had to manhandle you, too, didn't I?'

He waited for her to reply. When she remained silent he took her by the arm gently.

'If you've had enough air I'd better take you back. Actually, I've quite a lot of work to do.'

'Can I help you?' she offered quietly. 'I'm quite capable of running administration from my cell.'

He gave a smile. 'If you'd ever seen the inside of a North African prison you wouldn't look on your suite that way. Thank your lucky

41

stars I managed to get you bail.'

'I'm sorry,' she murmured. 'I shall never be able to thank you sufficiently for all you've done.'

'It's nothing,' he said stiffly. 'I'd have done the same for any member of my staff.'

He saw her to the door that divided her apartment from the office.

'I need things to occupy my mind,' he told her. 'If you can sleep with the occasional click of a typewriter next door, I think I'll use the office.'

'Why don't you let me help?' she pleaded. 'I need things to occupy my mind, too.'

He shook his head. 'Forget about hotel work while you've got this hanging over your head. When it's over we'll talk business once more. But I don't expect, for a moment, you'll ever want to see the inside of a hotel again.'

He wished her good night.

*   *   *

Settled behind the desk, Chris stared into space forlornly. There was little that required immediate attention. Stephanie had kept everything religiously up to date. But he needed an excuse to be near her, and yet on his own.

He ran a hand through his brown hair.

If any of his business friends could have seen him at that moment they would have wondered

42

what had happened to the hardbitten businessman. Where was the debonair playboy image?

He grew annoyed with himself.

Why had he come tearing out here, flying his own plane, dropping all other commitments? Had it been simply because an attractive girl had sounded odd on the phone?

Why should it worry him what became of Stephanie? She was a good-looking girl. But so were the mass of his staff. He employed attractive women to look after his concerns. They were good for business. He had found that out a long time ago from his father.

He gave a deep, miserable sigh.

Why fool himself? He had known for months that his feelings for Stephanie were greater than he cared to admit. He had felt it from the moment her aunt had introduced her and had tried to cover it.

It had inspired him to make her his first choice when the vacancy occurred at this hotel. It was a means of sending her away so that she wouldn't always be in his thoughts.

But the operation hadn't been a success. From the moment he'd returned to England he'd deeply missed her. It had only needed her phone call to bring him flying back.

And now it seemed as though it was possible that he would lose her for good. Inspector Abusaid seemed to have a reasonable case.

He whipped his thoughts into place.

No! Stephanie was innocent. If it came to a trial the jury would be sure to see that.

And after the case—what then? He would cut her out of his life. He couldn't afford to bind himself to a woman. He had seen the troubles they caused his associates. Marriage was not for him.

He locked that thought securely in his mind and left the room.

* * *

The following day brought an entirely unexpected development. During the morning Chris received a call from Inspector Abusaid. The man's urgent message sent him straight down to the police station.

When Chris returned his spirits were so high that he entered Stephanie's suite without even bothering to knock.

She looked at his boyishly enthusiastic face, waiting for him to speak.

'Keep sitting down!' he told her. 'I don't want you to have another fainting fit when I tell you some good news.'

Stephanie's heart pounded. She waited for him to continue.

'I've just come from Abusaid,' he went on. 'It seems that in spite of our friendship he's been covering some of the facts. Maybe that was the reason he had no objection to bail.

'Anyway, the post mortem has confirmed

everything. Solomon didn't die as a result of the lunge you gave him. He died much later— probably even as late as the next morning. He didn't even land at the bottom of the cliff below where you had the assault. It was about a hundred yards further on.'

He gave a shrug.

'Probably no one will ever know the real cause of death. It might have been suicide. But there's a greater likelihood it was a sheer accident. If he'd been wandering round in the dark it would have been an easy thing to miss his footing. And, I learned that above the point where he'd fallen, a piece of the path was missing. It had fallen into the sea . . .'

He stopped. Tears of relief were flooding the girl's eyes. For a moment he forgot the vow he had made the night before and held her close while she sobbed.

Then his voice grew husky. He drew away.

'Hurry up and get this over with. If you can get your suitcases repacked within the hour I'll get clearance for take-off. We can be back in England before you know where you are.'

*　　　*　　　*

After his small display of weakness, Chris was able to keep his emotions under control. He took command of the situation in his usual methodical fashion.

First, he promoted Margery to the long

45

awaited post of manageress. Although she was gossipy she had his best interests at heart. And she had been with the concern since his father's day.

Then he rang Constance, telling her the case had been dropped and they were flying back.

She received the news with relief and tears.

'I should wait at the flat,' he told her. 'The press is bound to get hold of the news. Arrange for the senior hostess to take over the club. Have a case packed and be ready to take Stephanie right away. Ring one of our hotels in Wales—the deeper in the wilds the better. Once the media tire of the story the hue and cry will die down.'

Later, he drove Stephanie to the nearby airport where his plane lay.

During the long flight home they had little conversation. Stephanie slept, making up for her past nights of sleeplessness.

When the small jet aircraft came down through a bank of cloud to touch down on the English runway she awoke. Remembering the past days, she gave a shuddering sigh of relief.

Chris came out of the pilot's cabin.

'Well—you're home!' he said breezily.

'Thank you,' she breathed.

A moment later she looked out of the window. A crowd of reporters and television cameramen came into view. They seemed to bear down on the aircraft.

Her heart quailed.

'Surely they didn't know about me in England!'

He replied without expression.

'Then you thought wrong. I've kept the English newspapers away from you. I'm sorry. Perhaps I should have warned you this might happen.'

She closed her eyes, self-pity overwhelming her.

'I'll never be free. Never. Wherever I go people will point me out. Perhaps a lot of them will even believe I *was* guilty of killing Solomon.'

He grew angry.

'What did you expect—that we'd get back here without anyone the wiser? Do you want jam on everything?'

He pulled himself up. 'Anyway—don't fool yourself. You'll be just another nine days wonder—nothing more. In a few weeks people will be wondering where they heard the name of Stephanie Hartland before. They'll have forgotten all about you.'

He looked deeply at her face. That would never happen in *his* case.

When they alighted from the aircraft he protected her as much as he could.

Pushing her ahead of him through the crowd, he shouted—'No comment! Would you mind letting Miss Hartland through? She's had rather a tough ordeal, as you probably know . . .'

47

In an hour's time, when he had deposited Stephanie safely at her aunt's flat, he left.

'I'll be in touch sometime,' he murmured.

Stephanie watched him go. Her mind felt numb.

Constance took her cold hand. Her heart went out to her. The girl had lost weight. And a look of fear seemed to haunt her eyes.

It had been true. Stephanie had been through hell. Chris had been sensible to suggest taking her right away. It was quite on the cards she would suffer a breakdown. The terrible experience she had had would take a long time to brush away.

CHAPTER FIVE

The early October sky was beginning to show signs of autumn. The first leaves were falling as Stephanie and her aunt came back from their walk in the woods.

A month had passed since Chris had brought her home. She had recovered outwardly from her ordeal. The few pounds she had gained in weight accentuated her good looks.

Nobody in the hotel had recognised her as the girl involved in the North African incident. Immediately after Chris had left, Constance had driven them to one of his less popular hotels in Wales. Tucked away in the countryside, there was less likelihood of her being identified. At that time of year the hotel was getting ready to close down for the winter break.

She had let none of the staff into her secret. Registering them both in the name of Reed, Stephanie's surname was safely forgotten. She would have to be known by her new name from now on.

Constance had written to Chris conveying both their thanks for all he had done. But he had not replied. Neither had he phoned. She had deemed it wise. It was better that the hotel didn't connect them with its owner.

She glanced at her niece now, as they neared the hotel drive. She was relieved to see that her haunted look had flown. For a long time the girl had been inclined to jump at her own shadow.

She smiled affectionately. Their break in the countryside had been the best medicine anyone could have prescribed.

Constance spoke thoughtfully. 'I really feel that I ought to contact Chris and find out if he wants me back at the club.'

Stephanie glanced at her. The thought of returning to London filled her with mixed feelings.

'But I'm sure you should stay on here until the hotel closes,' her aunt went on kindly. 'All this has done you so much good.'

'I can't stay here for ever,' Stephanie

shrugged. 'Any rate—we can't afford it.'

Her aunt laughed. 'There's no question of that. Chris will reimburse us. We've only to put in our claims.'

Stephanie spoke quickly. 'I can't possibly do that. Chris Denning has done enough for me. And I'm not even sure if he wants to go on employing me. Or even whether I want to stay with his concern.'

Constance looked at her sadly. 'I can understand that—after all you've been through. But what else would you do?'

Stephanie gave a sigh. 'I'm not sure. Father never prepared me for very much. It didn't seem necessary at the time. I never realised he was in such debt until after his death.'

'But you're good at hotel and club work,' her aunt pointed out. 'If you don't go on working for Chris I think you should take up something in that line. It gives you a home, too.'

Stephanie made no reply. Each time they spoke about Chris she experienced a feeling of pique over her muddled feelings.

When she had first met him she had disliked him. She had been always aware of his reputation. Gradually, that dislike had turned to a feeling of attraction that she had done her best to hide. She didn't fancy becoming like the rest of the hostesses.

Later, in North Africa, she had begun to see a different side of him. He had been kind and helpful—a true and loyal companion. If it hadn't been for him she might have been in Inspector Abusaid's jail even now.

But, on their return home, he had shown a complete lack of interest. All that they'd built up had gone. Curiously it hurt.

What had made matters worse was the conversation she had heard in the hotel this morning.

Two of the reception staff had been tittering behind the desk. She had overheard Chris's name being mentioned in connection with a manageress of another of his hotels.

'Silly little piece!' one of them had said. 'Doesn't she realise that the boss always tests out his staff before he launches them on the general public. It's part of the perks, isn't it? If she can say "no" nicely without slapping his face then she gets top marks. But the trouble is that very few can say "no" to Chris Denning. I bet he's found that out for himself a few hundred times!'

Stephanie had searched her heart. Had she ever given him the impression that she was that kind of person? She remembered the time she had clung to him, sobbing with joy that she was free. She had experienced a warm, safe feeling in his arms. It had continued even after he had abruptly disentangled himself.

She felt the colour increase in her cheeks.

No. It would be better not to work for Chris Denning any more. It was easy to become infatuated with someone who had saved your life.

He was a womanizer. If she fell in love with him it would be only a passing affair on his side.

She surprised herself that she could bear to think about falling in love with anyone.

Chris's words came back to her.

'. . . you must think all men are made up of brute force and violence. I couldn't imagine you ever wanting anything to do with them any more . . .'

It was true to an extent. The physical side of a relationship repelled her. What she had endured from Solomon would haunt her for a long time.

She heard her aunt give a small cry of surprise as the car park of the hotel came into view.

'Well—speak of the devil! That looks like Chris's Rover. I would think my holiday's come to an abrupt end. He probably wants me back. I wonder why he didn't ring.'

Stephanie felt an excitement rise within in.

The manageress took Constance swiftly aside as soon as they entered. She gave her a knowing smile.

'Mrs Reed—I didn't realise you were a friend of my employer. He arrived here about a half an hour ago. I showed him to your suite. I hope that was all right.'

Constance looked back at her. By the woman's manner it was obvious that she thought she was another of Chris's girl friends.

She found the idea flattering. She was at least six years older than him. But he resembled his father. And, although he was now dead, she had never completely stopped loving him.

She gave the other woman a smile.

'Oh, that's kind of you. I hope you've given him some refreshment. If not, perhaps you'd arrange to send some drinks up straight away. I'm sure Mr Denning will want one after such a long drive.'

The manageress agreed readily. It wasn't often the boss paid them a visit. And never had he brought a girl friend there.

Stephanie felt her heart playing tricks as they took the lift to the first floor. But she had brought it under control by the time they reached their suite.

The door was open. She saw Chris before he saw them. He was standing by the window surveying the view.

He turned at the sound of their footsteps, coming forward to meet them. His eyes were on Stephanie as he kissed her aunt briefly on the cheek.

'It's nice to see you both looking so well,' he remarked.

He made no attempt to kiss Stephanie.

'How are you?' he asked, putting out his hand.

For a moment she felt the warmth of his handshake. Her hand remained in his until she released it quickly.

'I'm much better,' she replied.

Her aunt was chatting about their carefree holiday, saying it looked as though Chris could do with one, too.

She ended by saying, 'I presume you've come to ask me to go back to work.'

He gave a short laugh.

'You've guessed right. But let's talk about that in a while. Tell me—has a month been enough for you, Stephanie? I've no desire to drag you away from all this Welsh scenery. It makes me realise what I miss, stuck away in the Metropolis. I almost wish I could spare a few days leave of absence for myself. Having been born in the country, I suppose I'm still a country lad at heart.'

Constance laughed. 'I doubt it. You're too much like your father. I could never imagine *him* burying himself in the wilds.'

'Oh, but he did,' Chris was quick to remind her. 'For a whole year, when I was a teenager, my father stayed at our country home. It was while I was recovering from a period of illness. I had the stupid idea that he was staying because of me. But I was sadly disillusioned. He'd fallen deeply in love—probably for the first time in his life.'

'I never knew about that,' Constance replied shakenly.

'My dear woman—don't blame yourself. I hate to shatter any of your illusions but it had nothing to do with you. It was to do with our latest housekeeper. I found that out much later. She eventually turned the tables on him. He probably richly deserved it after all the hearts he'd broken. But it altered his character. You may have noticed. He was never the same person again.'

Constance nodded. Geoffrey had died still virtually a young man. It had shocked them all.

'I never realised,' she murmured. 'Poor Geoffrey!'

Chris's tone lightened after the waitress had brought them their drinks. He began to talk about his reason for coming.

'Actually, I came to offer you both a proposition. Would it hurt you very much if you didn't come back to the Sunflower Club, Constance?'

She stared back at him with disbelief.

'I'm not sure what you mean . . .'

He laughed. 'I'm not thinking of sacking you. I'm sounding you out to see if you'd like a change of scenery. You must be sick of the same old faces. You've been running the club for years. I thought you might like a break.'

'That depends what it is,' she murmured. 'I've got used to that type of clientele. I can't say I'd be over the moon about managing anything like this.' She stared about at the less ornately furnished surroundings.

Chris shook his head. 'No—that's not what I had in mind. I'm not sending you out to grass. There are many people capable of running a

55

hotel like this. I want you—and Stephanie—for something quite different.'

Stephanie showed interest. He examined her reaction without it being noticeable.

'Some months ago I bought a rather nice manor house and lodge—not too far away from here, as a matter of fact. I've been having alterations made to it. It was once the home of Sir Humphrey Noall. But now it's unrecognisable. I've turned it into a country club—much to the chagrin of some of the villagers.

'It's almost ready to open. It'll be run on similar lines to the Sunflower Club, but with the added advantage of rural amenities. I think it could go down big once it gets going.

'I've been pummelling my brains as to who I think could best run it with the right amount of suave assurance and grace. And I've picked on you, Constance—with the help of Stephanie. I thought you might like to work together again. I didn't want to lay too much responsibility on Stephanie until she'd gained confidence. I think you're the best teacher.'

Constance considered.

She was immensely flattered that Chris has given her first opportunity to refuse. Although she was one of the most experienced of his manageresses, she knew she was also one of the oldest. He could so easily have chosen a younger, more attractive woman. And he had, in a way, by making Stephanie her assistant.

She smiled. 'I think it would be nice to have a change. But I really think you should ask Stephanie what she thinks. We had a little talk on our way home. I believe she's very undecided at this point as to whether she wants to stay with the concern.'

Stephanie felt his eyes on her. She found herself floundering.

'I didn't think you'd want to go on employing me.'

'Why ever not?' Chris's manner was sharp.

He'd been aware of how much more attractive she'd become. It had almost taken his breath away when she'd entered the room. During the last month he'd succeeded in hardening his heart towards her. Now he felt himself weakening.

She went on. 'I haven't been with you long. And I've caused you a lot of trouble.'

'Forget that. It's all behind you. The media's forgotten you. I told you they would. And you have a natural ability for this kind of work. Don't think I want to go on employing you out of sympathy.'

His outspokeness confused her.

'I don't know,' she sighed.

He went on quickly. 'Naturally, I'd like you to see the place before either of you finally decide. It's not far from here. In the adjoining county—Shropshire. I shall be staying there tonight. Why don't you drive down and see it tomorrow?'

Constance grew suspicious. It occurred to her that he was bending over backwards in order to please them. Maybe, as she had at one time suspected, he had visions of making Stephanie his next conquest.

Her suspicions were allayed when he looked at his watch after staying with them only a short while.

'And now, I'm afraid I must leave you. I've a lot to arrange at Minton Spiers—that's the name of the place. I really shouldn't have taken the time off to come here. I should have rung. But, since I was so close, I thought a visit would be preferable to discussing this over the phone. I know a lot of staff inadvertently listen in. I also thought it would give me a chance to make myself known here. A lot of my smaller concerns get neglected.'

Before he left he gave them instructions for finding the new country club.

They accompanied him to his car.

'I think we should start packing now,' Constance said. 'Whichever way we decide it's time we went back. Stephanie's so much better. I don't think either of us will ever be able to thank you enough. Your idea about getting her away was the best tonic there was. Look at her now, with the roses back in her cheeks!'

Chris looked, before tearing his eyes away quickly and starting up the car.

As he drove off Stephanie was trying to come to terms with her aunt's statement. She had never realised the holiday had been his idea. She had thought it was her aunt's. It made her debt to him greater.

In bed that night she tried to analyse her true feelings for him. She found her findings disturbing. She was even more undecided as to whether to stay in his employ.

In the morning she was quiet as they drove off in her aunt's car. To still her mind she took in the scenery.

It grew softer as they entered Shropshire. She understood why Chris had chosen it as the setting of his new club. It had a freshness and romance lacking in some other counties.

The small village they drove through consisted of mainly black and white timbered properties. Some of the locals looked at them curiously when Constance stopped and asked for directions to Minton Spiers.

'If you're wanting Sir Humphrey Noall, he's moved to the modern house the other side of the bridge,' the shopkeeper told her.

'No—it's the new country club I want,' she replied.

Stephanie was quick to notice the villager's disapproval. The shopkeeper gave her aunt the direction with a sullen air.

'You can't miss it. Keep straight on. You'll see the lodge on your righthand side. It's got fine mullioned windows. I'm glad the new owner hasn't messed about with those.'

As they turned in the drive and passed the

lodge on the way to the larger house they met Chris.

Stephanie had wondered whether he'd been lying when he'd told them he was a country boy at heart. But his dress seemed to confirm it. He looked even more at home in his casual jeans and carefree sweater. The overall effect made her heart race, but she kept her feelings under a tight rein.

He looked pleased when he saw them.

'You found it all right then,' he smiled.

'No thanks to your directions,' Constance laughed. 'We had to ask again in the local shop. But the man's attitude I'd say you've struck some local opposition. He was barely polite.'

Chris shrugged. 'They'll grow used to it. They're all very fond of the chap who used to own it. But I think we can expect some good business all round once we're underway. Naturally, I shall give it a lot of publicity. It could end up as our biggest source of income. A lot of the clients who frequent the Sunflower Club will use this for holidays. Let me show you around.'

First he showed them the house. His voice held a mixture of pride and achievement. The inside of the manor had been converted to suit his needs but it still retained all its erstwhile grandeur.

Later he showed them the lodge.

'It's a little far from the house but I don't think that's a bad thing. I thought you might use it yourself as self-contained accommodation.'

Constance admired the architecture but not the furnishings.

'I should need carte blanche to put all this back in the hotel and bring down my own things,' she told him.

'Naturally. Since it would be yours you could do exactly as you wished.'

From the window of a bedroom, Stephanie looked out over the grounds.

'What are those over there?' she asked. 'They look like stables.'

Chris moved closer to her side.

'Yes, they are,' he confirmed. 'I'd been wondering what to do about those so I left them. There's ample room for car parking at the side of the house.'

She grew more enthusiastic.

'Is there a chance that they could be stocked for the convenience of the guests? If it's to be a country club it should have those kind of amenities.'

'Why not?' he smiled. 'I'm all for those kind of ideas. If you can find someone to run them I've no objection.'

'I might take them over myself,' she told him quietly.

Constance had followed them into the bedroom.

'I wouldn't have thought that was a very good idea, Stephanie,' she murmured. 'In view of what happened to your father.'

Chris looked back at her.

'What happened? You'd only told me he died under tragic circumstances.'

Constance put him into the picture.

'He died in a riding accident. I thought Stephanie would have told you.'

Stephanie's face was expressionless.

'There are a lot of things we have to get over in life,' she said quietly. 'I don't think that experience should stop me from riding again.'

Chris gave a smile of encouragement.

'I agree. No experience should put you off things for life. Why don't you give thought to the starting of a stable? I'd have no objection.'

His words made up her mind for her.

'Then I'd be happy to stay with your concern and help my aunt to run the new country club. Having horses would give me a spare time occupation.'

He grew elated, but covered it.

'Then that's all settled. We'll go up to the house and have a drink on it. I think the final alterations should be completed by the end of a couple of weeks. After that we'll have a gala opening of the Minton Spiers Country Club.'

CHAPTER SIX

It took several more weeks after the gala opening before Stephanie could give further thought to the starting of a stable at the club. In spite of the opposition from most of the villagers, the Minton Spiers Country Club seemed to grow into an overnight success. It was exciting for Stephanie to be in on one of Chris's projects right from the beginning.

He took a busman's holiday. For reasons of his own he had given more thought to this venture than to some of his others. It was a way of ridding her from his thoughts. But, in the end, he had found that impossible. And, from the moment he had seen her again his feelings had flooded back.

Now he stayed on, indulging his desire to be with her, but, using his own vibrant personality at the same time, to promote the popularity of the club.

Late one evening, before she went back to the lodge, he walked her around the grounds.

'I shall have to go back to London tomorrow,' he told her.

She experienced a stab of disappointment.

He kept his tone light. 'I've really given too much of my time to getting this venture off the ground. I don't think my presence here is necessary any longer. I think you and your aunt are quite capable of pulling in the customers on your own.'

'Will you be based at the Sunflower Club again?' she asked, trying to keep her interest from being too apparent.

'Only for a while,' he told her. 'It will probably be necessary for me to spend some time in France shortly. My associates and I are considering a merger with Madame Roget and her concerns.'

'Oh!' she replied.

Madame Yvonne Roget was well known from her photographs in the newspapers. Her escapades were as talked about as Chris's. She was a tall, willowy brunette, as attractive as any of the girls he employed as hostesses.

'Yes,' Chris went on. 'I shall be interested to meet her. It's not often one finds a keen business brain in the head of such a beautiful woman.'

Stephanie felt a sharp pang of jealousy at his words.

'I wouldn't have thought a merger was necessary,' she murmured. 'Your business is sound enough without one.'

Chris gave a laugh. 'Mergers—or partnerships—are very necessary sometimes. They can cement a hotel business like mine and make sure of international success.' He grew thoughtful. 'But I'm only mentioning all this in passing. I'd be glad if you didn't pass it on until everything's settled. The media's only too anxious to latch on to any tasty bits of news— as we both found out.'

Stephanie turned away. The North African episode now seemed ages past. She wished he hadn't reminded her of it.

She gave a shiver. He noticed at once.

'You're cold,' he said. 'You've come out without a coat. Here—take mine.'

He took it off and wrapped it round her shoulders.

As it touched her bare arms she felt the warmth of his body. It gave her greater comfort than the mere jacket.

'Let's walk over to the stables,' he suggested. 'You can tell me the plans you have for starting them up. I'm afraid I've given you little spare time lately to put them into action.'

She agreed, fearing the time when she would be on her own again.

Walking amongst the loose boxes made her remember a time when her life had been very different. As she became thoughtful Chris grew conscious of it. It made him feel locked out.

'Tell me a little about your life before you came to London to stay with your aunt,' he invited.

'What do you want to know?' she asked. 'I'd never done hotel work before, as you know.'

He studied her curiously. 'Yet you have an aptitude for administration. You must have done something in that line before.'

She gave a smile.

'I helped my father keep the books for his business. He bred horses. We had a largish stable. It was necessary to work out the animal feed and the amounts we could expect from sales of foals. We also had to account for fees for siring.' She laughed awkwardly. 'It was all very different from the ordering for a high class hotel. But yes—there was a certain amount of administration. My father was never very good at keeping books. His interest was more on the practical side.'

He watched her sadness grow as she told him about the sudden death of someone she had loved and admired.

'After his funeral I thought I might have been able to keep things running on my own, but it was out of the question. It appeared that he had greater debts than I'd ever known about. He must have worried about these in private. They were from long ago—before I was born and he first started the business. Interest had accrued. I'm afraid it ate into all of the capital remaining. Everything had to be sold to pay what he owed.'

She stopped suddenly. What she was telling this fabulously wealthy man at her side must sound so trivial.

He was looking down at her with an intense look in his eyes that captured hers.

She grew alarmed that his hypnotic gaze could make such a weak fool of her. Self loathing filled her to think how easily she could become another of his affairs. During the past few weeks with him constantly there it had been easy to forget the rumours that flew about him.

Chris was unaware of what she was thinking. He was only conscious of his own desire. He wanted Stephanie as he had rarely wanted anyone.

Pushing aside all the vows he had made to himself he took her hand and pulled her close to him. Stephanie's acquiesence made him bold. He took her into his arms and kissed her long and lingeringly.

Stephanie allowed herself the luxury of receiving what her heart craved.

Then she drew away.

She forced her voice to become cold. 'Just because you pay me a salary doesn't mean you can buy my favours, too, Mr Denning. You can count that kiss as exoneration of the debt I owe you, nothing more. I don't intend becoming like your other women staff. When I give my love it will be to someone worthy. And now— will you take me back—unless, of course, you'd like to sack me for gross insubordination?'

For several seconds Chris felt himself lost for words. The kiss she had seemed to return had left his head singing. The slow realisation that it had meant nothing more than the payment of a debt she thought she owed made him angrier than he had ever known.

He took her roughly by the arm, dragging her to the lodge. There he removed his coat from her shoulders.

His tone was like ice. 'Since you despise me so much, I can't think how you can bear to have anything I've worn so close to you.' He grew more furious. 'But you're perfectly right—I shouldn't feel the generous salary I pay you gives me access to your favours. You have my abject apology.'

She stared back at him. His words stung her like a whiplash.

'As to any debt,' he went on, 'there was none so far as I know. So it's actually *I* who have been overpaid. Goodnight, Miss Hartland—I mean—Miss Reed. I don't think it's likely I'll be back to the club until well into the new year. That should give us both ample time to forget what happened.'

Without noting her expression, he went swiftly away into the darkness.

*　　　*　　　*

In bed, Stephanie spent hours regretting what she had said. His kiss had come as something she'd longed for. It was only when she'd given way to her feelings that she'd become dreadfully ashamed of herself.

For the next week she fought desperately to forget about the incident. She decided, with more time on her hands, to go ahead with her plans to fill the stable.

She told her aunt about it one morning when they had had their discussion about menus and the dinner dance taking place that evening.

Her aunt smiled.

'Chris should be pleased that you're taking such an interest in making the club a success.'

Stephanie resisted the desire to talk about him.

'It'll be for my own satisfaction, too,' she said quietly. 'It'll be nice to have horses around the place again.'

Her aunt nodded sympathetically before an idea struck her.

'Wouldn't it be better to lease the horses first? If, by any chance, the amenity doesn't catch on, it will save us the bother of selling them afterwards.'

Stephanie didn't see, herself, how the idea could fail. But she listened to what Constance had to say.

'There's a man about a couple of miles from here. His name's Gareth Hunt. I heard a client talking about him a few evenings ago. Apparently he has horses. You could call in there after you've picked up the flowers I ordered from town.

'It would give you a little bit of a break, too. I've noticed you've been looking a bit peaky these last few days. It doesn't do to throw yourself too wholeheartedly into your work. We've still got Christmas to get through. And it looks as though we're going to be frenetically busy. We're already overbooked. I'm praying we'll get a few cancellations.'

Stephanie considered her words. It wouldn't do any harm to see this man. She had to start somewhere.

On her way back from the town, the rear of her aunt's estate car filled with flowers for the decoration of the hotel and dance area, she stopped on the other side of the village at the Hunt premises.

Leaving her car at the edge of the road, she walked up the drive.

Noises from the stables ahead brought back a hundred bitter sweet memories. She resisted the temptation to visit them first before she called at the nearby house.

As she knocked, the sound of a conversation reached her through an open window at the side. A young woman was speaking with irritation.

'Why won't you recognise the fact that I'm an adult? I'm eighteen next week. It's about time you and grandfather stopped treating me like a kid!'

She heard a man reply.

'Stop trying to grow up too soon. What's wrong with being a kid?'

'Everything!' the girl wailed. 'You can't seem to realise that I've got a heart and feelings. They're nothing like a kid's, I can assure you.'

Stephanie, with her hand on the knocker, became embarrassed. It was obvious she was breaking into an argument. She wondered whether she should leave her mission till another time.

But the young man who was standing near the window suddenly observed her. A look of relief came into his eyes. He came immediately to the door, greeting her as though she was a long lost friend.

She felt her hand gripped in his the minute the door was flung open.

'Why, Miss Reed, this is an unexpected pleasure. How are you and your aunt settling in? I've been meaning to call and pay my respects and sample some of your hospitality. But, apparently, you've beaten me to it. Won't you come in?'

Stephanie covered her surprise. She and the young man had never met before. She was astounded he knew who she was.

'That's kind of you, Mr Hunt. But I can't stay long. I have to get back to the club. I've called on business. I hope you'll be able to help me.'

His face wreathed in smiles.

'I'll do that willingly—providing it's within my power.'

He ushered her into his kitchen. It was the untidiest room she had ever seen.

A young woman was standing by the stove. She was attractive, but her face was marred by tears. She brushed them away quickly.

Stephanie pretended surprise at seeing her there. She thought it was as well to let her think she hadn't overheard their conversation.

'Oh, I'm sorry. I didn't realise you already

71

had someone here!'

The man laughed.

'Oh, this is only Alison. She finished school last term. She's Sir Humphrey Noall's grand-daughter. You probably haven't had a chance to meet each other yet.'

He introduced Stephanie to the younger woman.

'Alison—this is Miss Stephanie Reed from the new country club.'

Stephanie became aware of the girl's hostile glare. For a minute she was reminded of Anis.

She tried to give her a friendly smile but it wasn't returned. It made her feel awkward.

'Oh, look—I'm not going to interrupt you. I only came to discuss something my employer and I have talked about. There's no hurry. It can wait till another time . . .'

Gareth's insistence that she should stay was pointed.

'No, don't go, Miss Reed. Now that you've broken the ice by calling, I can't possibly let you go without offering you some refreshment. What on earth will you think of our village hospitality?'

Stephanie caught the look in the young woman's eyes again. It was still surly. Once more she was reminded of Anis. The girl's obvious dislike of her sparked her annoyance. She had done nothing to deserve it. A touch of stubborness made her change her mind.

'Very well. If you're sure I'm not intruding?'

Gareth gave a relieved smile. He turned quickly to the younger girl hoping to impress her with his concern for Stephanie.

'Alison, love—will you have a hunt in the parlour for some glasses? Or maybe we'd all better go in there. It's not very grand to entertain Miss Reed in the kitchen . . .'

Stephanie gave a laugh. 'Oh, look—I'm being a nuisance.'

He denied it forcefully. 'No—no—I've told you you're not.'

She felt herself grow more embarrassed. The younger woman's face had turned stormy. The man hurried on.

'Well, perhaps we'd better stay in here, after all. I'm not sure the parlour's too clean, either. Alison—the glasses, love! I think you'll find them in the cabinet. Here—take this!'

He threw her a none too clean tea towel. 'You might give them a bit of a dust before you bring them in.'

Stephanie watched the other girl leave, noting her obvious unwillingness to leave them alone together.

It occurred to her that the man probably had an ulterior motive for paying her such undue attention. It was obvious the girl was infatuated with him. Perhaps he was trying to put her off.

She allowed herself to become the unwilling tool in his scheme.

He pressed her into a chair. 'Do sit down. How are you finding business? Are you getting all the bookings you hoped for?

She sat down, removing a pair of his socks from the arm of the chair as he was switching off the kettle that had started to boil.

'Yes, I think we're going to have a very good season,' she told him shortly.

He kept their conversation flowing, talking to her over his shoulder too enthusiastically.

'That's fine. It's always tricky when you start something new. I'm glad it's going so well. It's nice to see the old place has had a face lift, too. Sir Humphrey wasn't able to spend that kind of money. He'd let the place run down—which was a pity in view of its architectural value . . .'

Alison entered the room again. Her voice was cold.

'If you don't mind—it's my grandfather you're talking about. And I always liked the house the way it was. I thought *you* did, too. If I remember, you opposed the planning permission like everyone else.'

Stephanie looked at him sharply. The man was unabashed. He took the glasses from Alison, ruffling her hair playfully.

'Oh, I'm entitled to change my opinion. You want to keep Marshbank just the way it's always been. You're behind the times. Selling the manor was the best thing your grandfather ever did. And now you've got a nice, warm modern house.

'Minton Spiers, the way Miss Reed and her aunt are running it, is going to be an asset to

74

the village. They already employ fifty times as many staff as your grandfather. And that can't be bad with every other person in the district out of work.'

He took a bottle from a cupboard, pouring them each a drink. Making a point of handing Stephanie hers first, he said to Alison condescendingly—'Now—watch that doesn't go to your head!'

Stephanie felt the girl's embarrassment. It made her sorry for her.

Gareth ignored it if he saw it.

'Let's drink to a long and happy stay in the village for you, Miss Reed,' he announced cheerfully.

Alison's silence was ominous. She put down her drink untouched.

'I think I'll be going,' she said quietly. 'I don't think it's fair to leave grandfather on his own since he's been ill.'

'Oh,' Gareth said. 'Wouldn't you like to see the new foal again before you go?'

She shook her head.

Stephanie's intuition told her that the girl was fighting back tears. She watched her leave, conscious still of her dislike. Her anger rose towards Gareth. It had been unfair of him to bring her so despicably into their quarrel.

It was noticeable to her the way he dropped his act immediately Alison left.

He turned to her in a far less friendly way.

'Well, Miss Reed, how can I be of assistance

to you?'

She fought back her displeasure.

'This is really just a loose scheme my employer and I have been discussing. We thought we'd like to try out a stable for the use of the guests. But, as my aunt pointed out, it might be as well to lease some hacks until we're sure the amenity is going to catch on.'

She watched his eyes turn to dark pools of ice and wondered what she had said to annoy him.

Hurrying on she said, 'I'm sorry. I'm afraid you may find what I'm going to ask a bit of a cheek. Perhaps I've been misinformed about you.'

He smiled with a touch of irony.

'Oh, no. Do go on. I think I know what it is. You want to know if I'll loan you a few quiet nags.'

His anger was clear. She rushed to placate him.

'Oh, no. I wouldn't expect you to loan them to us. We'd be quite prepared to pay you a good price for their hire.'

He brought their meeting to an abrupt end.

'Well, I'm sorry to tell you that none of my stock is all that quiet. I don't breed them that way.'

She was disappointed, and disturbed, as well, that she'd been misled about his business. Her aunt hadn't mentioned that he was a horse breeder.

But his manner forced away all thought of trying to apologise. She started to leave as gracefully as she could.

'Oh, then it appears I've had a wasted visit. That's a pity.'

He allowed her to leave without making any attempt to stop her. But curiosity and a demon of hurt pride made her anxious to visit his stables.

She turned.

'While I'm here I wonder if I could have a look at your stock? I know a little about horses. I'd be interested to discover if they're as lively as you make them sound.'

Gareth looked back at her without expression. If Stephanie could have read his mind she would have known she'd guessed right about his former treatment.

He had used her to stop Alison from getting romantic notions about him. As far as he was concerned, she was still just a child. Albeit an extremely attractive one.

But Gareth knew his place. His ancestors had worked for the Noalls. There could be no question of him ever marrying the girl.

His feelings for Stephanie and her kind were a different matter. They had come to the village, trying to turn it into another suburb of the city. What right had they to start a country club in the area? It had been his, and the likes of his for centuries.

But, interest in his stock was hard to resist.

They were his pride and joy. He had worked up the business from nothing. Now he was a fairly wealthy man.

He took her up on her interest with a show of reluctance, leading her to the adjoining stables. With the arrogance of a self-made man he showed her the best of his stock.

Stephanie felt misgivings. The horses were a lot better than she'd expected. All at once she understood the man's nettled feelings at her calling them hacks.

But his behaviour still rankled. He had allowed Alison to leave in anger—most of it directed towards her. It was unjust.

She decided to take him down a peg or two. Stopping in front of the stall of a particularly high spirited horse, she patted its nose.

'This one looks quiet enough!'

Gareth studied her with amused surprise.

'Then it's easy to see you know little about stock. Orion happens to be the liveliest of the bunch.'

She gave a deprecating laugh.

'Oh, you'd hardly think so.'

He felt his anger rise. It would be pleasant to teach this haughty young woman from the city a lesson she wouldn't forget. To ride Orion she would have to be an expert. And he doubted if she was that. She was far too goodlooking—far too elegant in her well cut slacks and lace blouse. And far too superior.

'He seems so sweet and placid,' Stephanie

78

went on, disregarding the aggressive look in the stallion's eyes. 'I think you were only teasing me, Mr Holt.'

Gareth took her words as a challenge.

'Oh, so you think you'd be able to ride him, do you?'

'I know so,' she replied. Rubbing the nose of the fiery animal, she reverted to baby talk. 'You wouldn't tip me off, would you, my pet?'

Gareth grew incensed. He succumbed to great temptation. A mild fall in the adjoining meadow would do this stuck up female all the good in the world. He'd see to it that she didn't come to too much harm.

'Then perhaps you'd like to try him out?' he asked.

She seized his offer, ignoring the defiance in his tone.

'Of course. There's nothing I'd like better.'

Gareth summoned two of his stable lads harshly. 'Saddle up Orion and Casper for me, please. And make it snappy.'

The two boys rushed to do his bidding. It wasn't often they heard their employer display irritation.

Stephanie watched them saddle Orion, the black stallion, last. It was easy to see he was difficult to handle.

Gareth led him into the meadow himself, allowing the stable lads to bring Casper, the hunter he usually rode.

He gave a smile of sarcasm to Stephanie as

79

he closed the gate behind him.

'Well now, Miss Reed—maybe you'd like to put Orion through his paces.'

A moment of repentance stirred him as he looked down at her slender form. Orion would throw her almost as soon as she was in the saddle. He gave her a last chance to back out.

'If you'd like to think again, I'll take him instead and you can take Casper.'

She gave a careless shrug. 'No—I think I'm quite capable of handling him.'

Gareth regretted his weakness.

'Very well, then,' he said gruffly. 'Don't say I didn't warn you.'

One of the stable lads helped her into the saddle while he restrained the spirited animal's head. Then they stood back.

As soon as the horse was let go he took off like the wind. Gareth climbed immediately on to the less aggressive horse.

Stephanie had taken the sudden unleashing of power well within her stride. She had known the strength of the animal from the very first moment she'd set eyes on him.

Keeping her seat with a balance that came naturally from her years of working with horses, she resisted all the stallion's attempts to force her over his neck. With an iron will she used her expert knowledge to control him.

After she had shown him she was master, she pulled him up, forcing him to go at a slower pace. As soon as he obeyed she gave him his head again.

Gareth looked on, his apprehensions swiftly turning to admiration.

Stephanie put the beast into a gallop. Then, after a hundred paces, she restrained him in a canter. She seemed unaware of her audience, but Gareth could tell she was enjoying herself. He began to alter his opinion of her. She was a woman after his own heart.

When she had had all the excitement she craved, she put the beast into a regulated trot. With dignity, she took him out of the meadow and back to the stable, handing him over to a groom.

Gareth followed. His lads were looking on with suitably impressed expressions.

Stephanie started to leave quickly. Already she felt ashamed of herself. She hadn't meant to show off, only to teach the young man a lesson.

He accompanied her silently to her car. When they reached it he asked—'Where did you learn to ride like that? It wasn't in the city, I'll be bound.'

She gave an embarrassed laugh. 'Hardly— but then I wasn't brought up in the city. I had an entirely different existence before I joined Mr Denning's concern.'

He looked at her with interest. 'Tell me more!'

She bowed her head, giving a small shrug. 'Like you, Mr Hunt, my father bred horses, too.

81

I was brought up to eat, drink and talk horses from morning till night. It would have been almost sacrilegious if I hadn't learned to ride them as well.'

His anger towards her had long since flown. He wanted to learn all about her.

'And where was that?'

She grew reticent. 'At Newbury in Berkshire,' she told him shortly.

She noticed his smile of contrition.

'Then I think I've made a bit of a fool of myself, haven't I? I wanted to teach you a lesson for calling my horses hacks. But it seemed you very professionally turned the tables on me. Maybe you were right to call them hacks after what you've been used to.'

She became instantly apologetic.

'No. It was unforgivable of me. But I'd been misinformed about you. Your stock is excellent. I apologise for anything I've said to hurt you.'

Gareth met her eyes. He felt his feelings undergo a swift change. He wanted to please her.

'Look—I'd like to help you with your scheme. If you leave it with me I'll see a friend of mine. It's possible I can pick up some hacks cheaply.'

He waited for her reaction. It came with a ready smile that warmed his heart and built up his confidence.

'Maybe I can call and see you at the club in a few days' time?'

She agreed. Before getting into her car she held out her hand.

'You're being extremely kind to me, Mr Hunt. I don't really deserve it after that display.'

'My name's Gareth,' he reminded her. 'We don't stand on ceremony in Marshbank as you'll soon find out when you get used to us. Maybe I can call you Stephanie?'

She pulled her hand away quickly. She didn't want the man getting romantic ideas. She had no interest in him other than as a fellow horse lover.

He noticed her slight embarrassment and wondered whether he'd gone too far. He decided he had. The young woman was still mixed up with that hoity-toity lot. The two of them could never mix.

He started to walk back to his stables.

Stephanie regretted her foolishness. The man could help her. She gave a toot of her horn, attracting his attention before she drove off.

The man turned. She smiled at him again.

'I hope I'll see you at the country club soon, Gareth!' she called out.

He felt a sudden exultant feeling rise like a traitor within his breast. For a long while after the car disappeared from view, he stood thinking about her.

CHAPTER SEVEN

When Stephanie returned to the club she experienced a small feeling of jubilance that her scheme was beginning to rise from the planning board. It showed when she told her aunt about her meeting with Gareth.

Her aunt misread it. 'From the sound of it you two got on very well together.'

Stephanie flushed. She grew ashamed that she had used her attractions in such an underhand way to placate Gareth before she had left.

'I've no interest in men,' she replied sharply.

Constance smiled. 'You'll get over that one day. I'm sorry for teasing you. Anyway, he sounds as though he could be quite useful. I look forward to meeting him.'

It was the following day that she was given the chance. A horse truck pulled up in front of the hotel. Gareth got out of the driving seat.

Constance was the first to notice him from the window of her office, where she was discussing business with her niece.

'Who's that dish of a man?' she remarked.

Stephanie went to the window, following her gaze. She gave a delighted smile.

'Why, it's Gareth. And he's got some horses.'

Constance raised an amused eyebrow.

'He didn't waste much time! *You* may not have an interest in the opposite sex, but I

84

certainly think you've made a conquest where he's concerned.'

Stephanie ignored her comment.

'I'll go and see what he's got,' she said. 'I didn't expect him to bring anything so soon.'

She met Gareth as he strode into the reception area. He looked around with interest. When he saw her his face lit up.

She went forward and shook his hand.

'Welcome to Minton Spiers Country Club!'

He smiled and indicated the alterations. 'The old place looks very different.'

'I imagine it does,' she said. 'But I didn't see it before.'

'Oh, it's definitely an improvement—but don't tell Alison I said so. I'm afraid the place had fallen into a very bad state of repair. If the old man hadn't sold it it would have eventually tumbled round their ears.'

'Then you weren't really opposed to the planning permission?'

He looked at her awkwardly. 'Oh, yes, I was. And I suppose I still am in a way now. But there's nothing anyone can do.'

She challenged him with a smile. 'I thought you told Alison we were an asset to the village?'

He grew embarrassed. 'I was afraid you'd remember that. Perhaps some day I'll explain about yesterday.'

Her eyes twinkled. 'I'm going to be here for quite a while. There'll be plenty of time.'

She pointed to the truck outside.

85

'You've been good enough to bring me some horses by the look of it. I'm dying to see them. Can we take them down to the stable block?'

She followed him into the courtyard.

'I picked each one out myself,' Gareth explained. 'I don't think there's room for complaint. There's none of them that'll break the sound barrier. But I picked them up as reasonably as I could for you.'

She thanked him, getting into the passenger seat of the truck and directing him towards the row of loose-boxes they had had restored.

Gareth was impressed when he saw them.

'You've made a fine job here. From what I can remember they were in an even worse condition than the house. Your employer seems to spare no expense. He must be extremely wealthy.'

She had no wish to talk about Chris. Even the mention of his name sent a pain through her heart.

'Yes, he's a very successful businessman,' she murmured.

Gareth noted her reticence and stored it in his memory. Everything about this girl aroused his interest as it had never been aroused before.

When he took the four horses out of the truck he watched her face light up again.

She examined each one with a professional eye.

'But they're good, Gareth!' she exclaimed.

86

He gave a laugh. 'They're still what I call hacks.'

She made a face, remembered her terrible *faux pas* of the day before.

'You're never going to forgive me for that, are you?'

His laugh faded.

'Oh, yes. I forgave you yesterday—otherwise I wouldn't have taken the trouble to help you.'

She dropped her gaze. She was being careless in her treatment of him. It was easy to see he was attracted to her. She would have to tread carefully if she didn't want to hurt him.

After they had got the horses into their stalls Gareth asked her what she was going to do about their welfare.

'I presume you've got someone lined up to look after them? I doubt if your work leaves you all that much time to care for them yourself?'

She shook her head.

'No, not yet. I didn't expect you to turn up so soon. I shall have to get on the line to the employment agency.'

'Maybe I can help. I know a few youngsters who could do with a part time job. Looking after four horses isn't going to be a full time occupation. But it'll give an interest to someone who's still at school.'

She thanked him. 'That would be fine. I'd hoped to be able to do it all myself. But it's not always possible. There are times when I have to put in many more hours than normal. I expect Christmas will be one of those. We're already booked to capacity.'

'Then I'll see what I can do.'

She felt his warm brown eyes take in hers. Her liking for him grew.

Later she brought him back to meet her aunt.

Constance settled Gareth's account, which was minimal. He refused to accept the handsome commission she offered him for his services.

'I'm afraid you've received some stick from the locals about your presence here,' he told her. 'Maybe this will make up for it. We're slow about receiving strangers into our midst. But, when we do, we try to be lavish with our hospitality. I'll see word gets around that the alterations have been done sympathetically. I think you'll find that people will start to change their behaviour towards you from now on.'

After he'd gone Constance turned to her niece.

'What a charming person,' she told her. 'I think you could do a lot worse than cultivate an interest in that young man—when you find an interest in the opposite sex again.'

Stephanie pushed her remark aside. She was only interested in Gareth as a friend. Anything more was completely impossible while she told herself she was still in love with Chris.

Her employer's name came up in

Constance's next breath.

'Oh, by the way—I had a phone call from Chris while you were talking horses with the delectable Gareth. He was ringing from Paris. He wants to make sure we have a spare suite for over the Christmas period.'

Stephanie felt her heart pound. She hadn't expected him to return so soon. When he had left that night in anger he had mentioned not seeing her until 'well into the new year'.

Her aunt missed her heightened colour.

'I told him I'd see what I could do. I mentioned we'd made a mistake with the bookings and that we were praying for cancellations. I even offered to put him up with us at the lodge. But he said the suite wasn't for himself. It was for Madame Roget. Apparently he's been staying with her in her magnificent club in Paris.'

Stephanie remembered the merger he'd told her about before he'd left.

'Anyway—' her aunt was continuing—'he told me to make a cancellation if we hadn't got one. It was important that Madame Roget stayed here. As for himself, he jumped at my offer to make room for him at the lodge.'

When Stephanie went down to the stable later that day she viewed the future with misgivings. Christmas wasn't all that far away. Seeing Chris again so soon was going to be purgatory.

Dressed in her oldest clothes, she set about

the task of mucking out the horses' stalls. Afterwards, she groomed each one with care. Then she polished the tack Gareth had included in the sale to a brilliant shine.

Engrossed in her work, which she found relaxing and enjoyable, she felt her problems start to fade. It was as she was clearing up that she heard footsteps ring on the flagstones outside the loose boxes.

She went out of the tackroom to see who her visitor was. Hopefully, it might be the lad Gareth had promised to send up. She had been trying to work out how she could exercise four horses herself the following morning.

The auburn-haired young woman who was peering into the first stall looked vaguely familiar. She had her back to her. As soon as she turned Stephanie saw that it was Alison Noall. Her heart dropped.

Alison's attitude was still the same as it had been when she had met her at Gareth's. There was no friendliness in her expression. Stephanie waited for her tell her why she'd come. When the girl spoke it was in an offhand manner.

'I happened to hear you were looking for some part time help with the horses.'

Stephanie tried to smile. But it wasn't easy. The girl made her feel uncomfortable.

'That's right. Did Gareth send you?'

The girl was honest enough to shake her head, denying it.

'No way! I never want to speak to him again. Perhaps you'd noticed we'd been having a row.'

Stephanie told a lie. 'No, I can't say it was noticeable.'

The girl gave her a look of disbelief.

'Well, it doesn't matter.' She dropped the subject at once. 'Anyway—is it true you could do with some help or not? I'm used to handling horses. Gareth's taught me all I know. And I'm strong. It's necessary when you handle the sort of stock he's got. Maybe he introduced you to Orion?'

Stephanie relaxed. 'Yes, I rode him yesterday. He can be quite a handful.'

The girl broke the silence that followed. Her green eyes delved into Stephanie's.

'Well—do I get the job? I've given you my credentials. Is there anything else you'd like to know? Oh, by the way—I know the estate pretty well here—the bridleways—best paths for beginners—all the terrain. But then, of course, since I used to live here, I would, wouldn't I?'

Stephanie fought for a way out. It would be a dreadful mistake to employ the girl. They woud never get on together. She tried to get out of it diplomatically.

'Gareth mentioned you'd just left school. Surely you're going on to college or university?'

Alison gave her a look of dry amusement.

'Whatever gave you *that* idea? I'm no academic. I'm what's known as not terribly bright—according to my final report. I'm more interested in doing than thinking.'

'But surely you'll train for something?'

'There's no need,' she returned sourly. 'We're not hard up any more now that we've sold your employer our house.'

'But you can't just stay at home without doing anything!'

Alison took full advantage of the opening.

'I realise that. That's why I want the job you're offering. The money's not important. I'll even do the work for nothing, if you like.'

Stephanie felt as though she'd been pushed into a corner. It was necessary that she had someone to help her as soon as possible. It was on the cards that Gareth might not send anyone suitable for several days.

'Very well,' she breathed. 'We'll take out a couple of horses. I'll let you have my decision when I see how you handle them.'

Alison tacked up Swallow. It was clear that she knew what she was doing. Stephanie felt herself all fingers and thumbs as she put a girth around Yellowjack.

Night was drawing in as they returned from their ride in the meadow some distance away. There was no question that the girl was a competent horsewoman. Stephanie couldn't have chosen a better person to see that the horses were taken care of. But still she felt herself demurring.

As they put the horses back in their stalls Alison gave her a questioning look.

Stephanie could see no way out of her dilemma.

'Very well. The job's yours if you really want it . . .'

'And I do,' the girl retorted sharply.

Stephanie gave a resigned sigh.

'Then I'll expect you to start in the morning. There'll be mucking out—grooming—feeding and some exercising. Although I'm hoping the guests will do a lot of that themselves.

'Shall we fix your hours from eight in the morning till twelve. It's possible I'll need you in the early evening as well sometimes? You'll have to give me your address and phone number.'

'That'll suit me,' the girl nodded.

'And now for remuneration,' Stephanie went on.

Alison gave a shrug. 'I've told you, I'm not fussy. I'll do the work for nothing.'

Stephanie gave a tight smile.

'I'm afraid Mr Denning wouldn't allow that. If you work for him you'll have to suffer the ignomony of being paid—just like the rest of us.'

The girl's proud features told her what she

was thinking.

'Very well, then. I don't mind becoming working class. It's no dishonesty. My father was a tradesman—as some of the villagers might tell you. I'm not completely out of the top drawer, Miss Reed. Maybe that accounts for some of my tastes.'

'You mean your liking for Gareth Hunt?'

The girl flushed. 'I hate and despise him.'

Stephanie's pity rose. 'That's only because he probably fails to see you as adult. Why don't you go easy on him? I'm sure he'll wake up to the fact one day that you're a very attractive young woman.'

The girl glared at her harshly.

'Thanks, Aunt Jane! I can sort my problems out myself. I don't need to consult your agony column.'

Alison left, still wearing her sullen look, and Stephanie was reminded once more of the Arab girl and her insane jealousy.

Later, as she changed at the lodge for her evening session in the hotel, misgivings about having given the girl the job swept over her.

Why had she entangled her life still further? As if she hadn't enough problems to contend with already. Maybe it was *she* who should consult an agony column.

CHAPTER EIGHT

Whatever Alison's feelings were towards Stephanie, it didn't stop her from arriving the next morning half an hour before time.

Stephanie observed her from her bedroom window while she was dressing. It was hardly light and the days were drawing in. December was approaching when the mornings were misty and sombre.

Stephanie usually arrived at the hotel at about half past nine. Her aunt followed later. Their times of duty depended on how late they had had to stay at the club the night before. They employed several hostesses. But often one of them would oversee whatever was taking place until the last of the guests or clients retired.

Jenny, the receptionist, greeted Stephanie as soon as she entered the foyer.

'Oh, Miss Reed—Mr Denning's just phoned. He says will you or your aunt ring him back urgently. It's about the suite. He wanted to make absolutely sure that it had been booked for certain.'

Stephanie felt her heart lurch. It wasn't like Chris to ring so early. He must know her aunt wouldn't be there.

'All right, Jenny. Will you get me his number? I'll speak to him from my aunt's office. By the way, have we had any cancellations?'

The girl shook her head.

'I'm afraid we haven't. People are still ringing to book up and I'm having to put them off. Chris Denning really went to work on the advertising, didn't he? What's he offering by way of extras? Nude dancing on the lawn?'

Stephanie felt in no mood for humour. As she opened the door of the office her legs were shaking. She sat down behind the desk, praying she could speak to Chris without her nervousness showing.

When the phone rang she lifted it slowly. A moment or two later she heard his voice.

'Hello—is that Constance?'

Stephanie fought to keep her tone neutral. 'No. It's Stephanie. My aunt's not here yet.'

'Ah, Miss Reed,' he returned acidly. 'How kind of you to return my call.'

'Jenny mentioned it was urgent. I believe it's to do with the suite you require for Madame Roget, isn't it?'

Chris snapped back, 'That's correct. How smart of you to keep *au fait* with names.'

'Constance mentioned the name to me yesterday when she told me about your call. You also mentioned it yourself the last time I spoke to you. How is your business going in that direction? Have you managed to complete everything to your satisfaction?'

His tone lightened. 'Yes—I've got everything stirring nicely in the mixing jar. That happens to be the reason I want this suite for Madame

96

Roget over Christmas. It's very important.'

'You've no need to worry,' Stephanie told him. 'If we don't receive a cancellation before then we'll have to write to put someone else off. I'll see that it's done very diplomatically.'

Chris was silent for a moment. When he spoke again his voice had sharpened. It came over with a sarcastic edge.

'Ah, yes—you're an expert at diplomacy, aren't you? On second thoughts, perhaps you'd better get your aunt to write the letter.'

His manner made Stephanie reply bitterly and without thinking.

'That's the pot calling the kettle black, isn't it? If you were more diplomatic about some of your friendships with women staff, rumours wouldn't fly so hotly around you.'

He took her criticism of him less angrily than she had anticipated.

'Oh, indeed—and you take all these rumours to heart?'

She felt she had given away her feelings too openly. She tried to cover what she'd just said.

'I'm sorry—I'm being extremely rude. Your affairs are none of my business.'

Chris agreed with her. 'That's perfectly true. Just as your affairs are none of mine. By the way—how is Gareth Hunt? Give him my regards when you next see him.'

Stephanie's surprise showed through.

'How do you know about Gareth?'

His laugh rang down the phone.

'Constance happened to mention him yesterday. I hope he's not going to set me back too much for the horses he brought over so quickly. Actually, it came as quite a surprise to me when she told me how well you'd got on together. You see, I was naive enough to think you didn't want anything more to do with men. Or perhaps I'm mixing you up with someone else—someone who had a very nasty experience in North Africa.'

He heard her sharp intake of breath and began to apologise immediately.

'I'm sorry. That was a swine of a thing to say. And, if it's any consolation to you, I shall bitterly regret having said it for a long time.' He paused. 'I think if we can't talk civilly to each other it's probably best if we don't talk at all. Goodbye, Stephanie. I'll see you at Christmas.'

She heard the blatant click as he replaced his receiver before her.

For a long while she sat recalling their conversation. Then she went over to the window.

The day looked glowering. A wind had risen, blowing down the last of the leaves. She felt it blow through her heart.

Why had Chris asked her to ring him? He must know his wishes concerning Madame Roget would be strictly adhered to. And why had she been foolish enough to make her jealousy over his affairs apparent?

She sighed, going back to the reception area.

98

The newspaper van had just delivered a large pile of papers and periodicals. Jenny was marking them off into orderly heaps. Stephanie picked one up. It was the periodical her aunt always took.

She flicked through it, trying to put her thoughts into order. Suddenly, a picture on one of its glossy pages caught her eye. It was a photograph of Chris and Madame Roget taken together. They were leaving the Frenchwoman's fashionable club in Paris.

After her eyes had taken in Chris's handsome features, she passed to the caption beneath. It was written in the usual flamboyant style of that particular magazine.

'MATCHING PAIR.
'Suave Chris Denning and beautiful Yvonne Roget preparing to leave Mercredi's. Rumours have linked their names in a possible merger.
'Can it be we can hope to hear of a more romantic partnership before long?
'Catch that look in Chris's eyes. It looks as though love might have captured the debonair millionaire at long last.'

Stephanie let the magazine fall. She picked it up and placed it on the reception counter with trembling fingers.

For the rest of the morning she threw herself into her work with more fervour than she had ever done before.

In the early afternoon she changed and went down to the stables. She was relieved that Alison had left. Amongst the surroundings she knew and loved she gave vent to her misery. For a long time she stayed in the tackroom, weeping angry tears over the news she had read.

She was so immersed in grief that she didn't hear a man's footsteps cross the stable yard. Gareth stood at the tackroom entrance, overcome with surprise as he heard her sobs.

Sympathetically he went forward and put his arm round her shoulder.

'What's up, Stephanie? Are you hurt?'

She glanced at him, snatching at a handkerchief to cover her eyes.

'Oh, go away, please! I didn't want anyone to see me like this.'

He remained where he was stubbornly.

'But you're upset. I want to know what I can do.'

She untangled herself from his arm. 'You can't do anything. So please go away. I came here to be on my own.'

He stood back. 'I don't feel like going away. I've only just come. So—don't mind me. Continue your cry. When you've finished I'll introduce you to the crowd of stable lads I brought with me for you to interview.

'All right, lads—' he shouted—'she'll be with you in a minute. She's just having a good cry!'

Stephanie whirled round. The area outside

the tackroom was bare. She looked at Gareth accusingly.

'Just my little joke,' he told her. 'I happened to learn already that you've employed Alison. I came over to see if she was getting in anyone's hair. By the look of it she has.'

Stephanie blew her nose, shaking her head fiercely.

'Alison has nothing to do with it.'

He looked relieved. 'I'm glad. Then, at the risk of getting my head snapped off again, I'll ask you once more. Is there anything I can do?'

She looked at him wearily. 'No. It's purely a private matter. I found out something rather upsetting earlier this morning. I've been bottling it up. I feel better now I've got some of it out of my system.'

He smiled. 'I'm glad. Being a woman has that distinct advantage over a man. If it was me I'd have to resort to something physical. Perhaps start a fight—or take a brisk ride. Do you fancy a ride, since I'm here?'

She refused. 'No, thanks. I don't think I've the energy for one now. I feel entirely drained.'

He examined her face. She still looked remarkably lovely in spite of the marks of her tears.

'Then maybe we should go for a drive. It would take you away from your work for a while. I can show you a few of the local landmarks. They're quite beautiful—even in winter.'

101

She glanced at her watch. It wasn't necessary to be on duty before six.

'Thanks. I think that might be quite nice.'

He smiled at her again, letting his fondness show through.

'Then come on. A drive to the Long Mynd will make you forget your troubles. It's been there since the beginning of time. It does one good to see something as large as that. It puts things into perspective.'

As he drove her along the attractive roads of his well beloved county he told her a little about his life.

'My ancestors were all Shropshire men,' he said proudly. 'They were tilling the soil as far back as the seventeenth century. I broke with tradition when I went into horse breeding. But it was the only thing I'd ever wanted to do.

'I don't suppose I shall ever be a millionaire like your employer. But I'm not exactly penniless.'

The Long Mynd came into view round the next corner. He pointed it out to her.

'There it is. Sometimes it looks like a sleeping beast. When I was a child my father used to tell me silly tales about it. He said that one day it would wake up and gobble all the people in the district. Then, he said, it would slide on—down the road to Ludlow, and eat up all the people until it got to London.'

He laughed.

'Sometimes I used to pray it would eat my

teachers. I was never really keen on school. I suppose it's because I'm not the book learning type. My skill lies in my brawn.'

The embarrassed way he talked about himself showed up his lack of confidence. Stephanie found herself growing more fond of him. It was a relief to have his company after some of the snobbish types who used the hotel.

Gareth stopped the car where they could get a good view of the surrounding countryside.

'Tell me about yourself now. I seem to have been using up all the air space. I find your life much more interesting than mine. A horse breeder's daughter turned hotel manageress. That's a fascinating combination. You can only be about twenty-one or twenty-two?'

She smiled. 'I'm twenty-five—nearly twenty-six. And I'm not really a very interesting person. My father died owing a lot of money, and his stock and land had to be sold. I went to London to stay with my aunt. And it was while I was there that I started to work for Mr Denning. He thought I had the right lines—so he put me on the pay role.'

'The right lines?' Gareth echoed with an amused look.

She blushed. 'I meant the right attributes.'

He teased her. 'From what I've heard about Chris Denning, I'd have said you were right the first time. Word has got round the village that he's quite a playboy. Some of the men are locking up their daughters.'

Stephanie didn't find his words funny.

'I don't care to discuss my employer's affairs,' she said bitterly.

Gareth had the feeling he had said the wrong thing. He changed the subject as quickly as possible.

'Look at that sleeping beast! Have you ever seen anything so majestic? If you've regained your energy let's take a walk to the top. I know a short cut. It won't take too long.'

She agreed. Gareth's mention of Chris had brought back all her misery. She hoped she could blow it away with the wind.

He took her hand as they climbed the steeper part of the slope. Feeling her hand held tightly in his gave her security and a mild comfort. When they reached the top the gale took her breath away.

'How about that?' Gareth roared above the wind. 'Doesn't that make all your troubles feel small?'

He teased her again. 'What would you do now, my girl, if the beast suddenly came to life?'

The way he said it, looking down at her with a smouldering look, made her feel apprehensive.

He went on affectionately. 'You'd do nothing. Because I'd protect you from it. I'd be quite good at protecting you, Stephanie. I've had a lot of experience.'

She looked back at him questioningly.

'How have you had a lot of experience?'

He laughed, throwing his wild hair back into the wind.

'I didn't mean with women. I'm sorry if it sounded like that. I meant with animals. They need quite a lot of protecting. Especially when they're small and vulnerable.'

She relaxed. Gareth wouldn't hurt her. If it hadn't been for her hopeless love of Chris she would have found a lot about him that was extremely attractive.

He took her fond smile for something else.

With a swift movement he took her into his arms. For a moment she felt herself crushed against his heart. Then his lips found hers.

The unexpected action took her off her guard. She experienced suffocation. It brought with it every lurid detail of her assault by Solomon.

She felt panic take over. Struggling out of his embrace she let out a scream. The wind seemed to take it up, sending it over the surrounding valley.

Gareth stared at her with surprise and apprehension.

'What the hell's the matter, Stephanie? I only kissed you!'

She came to her senses, realising how she must have startled him. Her own fear still showed in his eyes.

She broke down, covering her face with her hands.

'Oh, keep away from me! Please keep away from me!'

Gareth looked on helplessly until her sobbing had died away. Then he touched her gently on the arm.

'Shall we go down the hill? I think we've both had enough of the Long Mynd for one day.'

She nodded. He helped her back without speaking to the car.

When they were sitting in the Land Rover, he took a pipe from one of the compartments. After he'd lit it, he blew a puff of smoke out of the window before turning to her.

'I believe you know, Stephanie, that there isn't anything in the world I would do to hurt you. So, in that case, it wasn't my kiss that frightened you. It was something else. Would you like to talk about it?'

She looked back at him, wondering how she could ever have been afraid. He was taller and stronger than Chris, but, in his way, more gentle.

Shaking her head, she told him—'There's nothing to tell. I had a bad experience some months ago. I thought I'd got over it but haven't. Perhaps it will take a lot longer than I thought.'

He looked at her sympathetically.

'I think I understand. It must have been something very terrifying. In that case, I'm sorry I brought it all back.'

She dropped her gaze.

He went on quietly. 'I realise we've hardly had time to get to know each other. I've probably rushed things a bit. It's something I promised myself I wouldn't do. But, at least I hope I haven't ruined our friendship.'

She shook her head. It gave him more confidence to go on.

'I ought not to crave any more. But I can't keep what I feel for you a secret. I'm very attracted to you, Stephanie. I don't suppose that comes as any surprise.'

She stopped him from going on.

'I like you, Gareth—very much. But I'm afraid I can't give you hope of anything more.'

'Then I'll wait,' he said softly. 'That's really all I can do.'

*   *   *

When he left her later at the beginning of the drive, he didn't make any attempt to touch her.

'Ring me any time if you need me,' he told her.

She nodded gratefully.

'I'll drop by and see you sometime in the week,' he promised.

They waved to each other cheerfully before she went into the lodge.

Alison, who had seen them from the village street, dodged into the shrubbery to avoid Gareth as he drove out.

Her mind filled in all the missing pieces of the parting she had missed.

What had that woman been doing with Gareth? She had known from his behaviour that he fancied her. It had been her only reason for wanting the job at the hotel stables. It was a way of keeping her eye on them.

Stephanie's words came back. '. . . why don't you go easy on him? I'm sure he'll wake up to the fact one day that you're a very attractive young woman . . .'

Her face crumpled. The blonde bitch! It was the sort of thing she *would* say if she'd wanted him for herself all along.

Tears crept through her lashes. They slid down her cheeks. It wasn't fair that nothing in the world ever turned out the way she wanted. She breathed a deep sob of despair.

She had wanted Gareth ever since she could remember. She'd even been prepared to wait until she was twenty-one before telling him. Now he'd never want to hear it.

Her love for him had helped her through the more difficult patches of her life—the grief when her father had died—and later when her mother had left. It had even helped her when her grandfather had sold her beloved home. Now, she saw, it could never come to anything. Stephanie had stolen him away.

Her tears increased, swelling like rivers in full stream. She broke into a run. If she could run really hard her heart might stop beating.

She could fall into an inert heap and be run over by a car.

Anything—anything—would be better than this pain she had to bear. Death would be an immense relief. It would take away all her suffering.

CHAPTER NINE

When Christmas was only three days away Stephanie looked back on the past month with a touch of surprise. It had gone by much quicker than she'd anticipated.

Her friendship had grown with Gareth and she found his company a great comfort. Several times a week they had gone out together. Sometimes he'd taken her riding and, on one evening he'd taken her out to dinner.

Not once had their relationship gone beyond the bounds of friendship, although Gareth might have wished for more.

Stephanie kept out of Alison's way as much as possible. The girl was still sullen and bad-tempered, but she carried out her work in an exemplorary fashion. Occasionally she stayed on to assist guests.

Life, as the festive season approached, became busy at the hotel. It left Stephanie with little time for her beloved horses. She was grateful that she had Alison to rely on.

On the evening of the twenty-third, she saw Chris's Rover pull up outside the hotel. She had known the approximate time of his arrival and had been watching out for him. She felt her heart beat wildly beneath her short evening dress. An unconscious movement made her play with the string of pearls at her throat.

Stiffly, she stopped herself. She had rehearsed her meeting with him. There was to be no nervousness. She had to be cool but friendly. There must be nothing to show that she had ached for his visit.

Rumours in the newspapers and magazines had made much of the proposed merger. Conjectures flew that the good-looking man had already asked Yvonne Roget to marry him. Perhaps soon she would find out that truth for herself.

Chris came hurrying through the entrance door out of the rain with the beautiful Frenchwoman by his side.

Stephanie forced a smile to her lips as she went to greet them.

'Good evening, Madame Roget—good evening Mr Denning. I hope you both had a good journey in spite of the weather. I understand it's pouring all over the country. I hope you'll find the warmth in the club sufficient. If not, I do hope you'll tell me. I'm afraid we've had a little difficulty with the central heating.'

Chris looked at her sharply. He ran a

practised eye over her appearance. She was still every bit as lovely as his heart remembered.

The colour of her gown exactly matched the deep blue of her eyes. But, at the moment they seemed cold, and wouldn't meet his.

He grew annoyed. He'd hoped she'd forgotten their feud. It brought out sarcasm in his tone.

'Good evening, Stephanie. You can drop the patter if it's for our benefit. Save your spiel for the guests. I've already told Yvonne what perfect manners our hostesses have.'

Stephanie looked down.

The Frenchwoman was quick to spot the blush that appeared in her cheeks.

She patted Chris's arm, reproaching him in a soft, attractive accent.

'What a horrible man you are! You have made the girl upset.' She threw Stephanie a condescending smile. 'I wonder why any of you stay with him. I think his manners are atrocious. Perhaps soon I shall see that your working conditions are improved. When Mr Denning is in residence I'll provide him with a muzzle.'

Stephanie met her eyes for a second. They seemed cold and extremely calculating. But she was every bit as attractive as her photographs, though slightly older. Nevertheless, she still retained all the beauty of a young girl. Her complexion was dew fresh and her dark hair gleamed as though it had been polished.

Constance caught sight of the three of them as she came through from the restaurant. She greeted Chris with warmth. He introduced her to Madame Roget.

When they had passed the usual small talk he brought the pleasantries to an abrupt end.

'Constance, I wonder if you'd mind showing Madame Roget personally to her suite. I'm sure she's longing for a hot bath. And Stephanie—I think you'd better accompany me to the lodge and let me know where I'm to stay. I don't want to commandeer someone else's room.'

She agreed, but her expression told her reluctance.

Outside, in the blustery weather, the porter was unloading Madame Roget's luggage. It filled the car boot.

'The small holdall's mine,' Chris told him, taking it and throwing it into the back seat. 'Get in the front,' he told Stephanie. 'We'll drive back to the lodge. I wouldn't dream of letting you walk in this.'

As soon as the porter had closed the boot, Chris turned the Rover with skill and speed. A few moments later he had parked it in front of the lodge.

He took the keys of the front door and saw her quickly in.

The moment he entered he noticed that the sitting room had been arranged with care.

None of the furniture that he'd left had been allowed to remain. But not all of the things he recognised as having been in Constance's flat.

'Very nice,' he approved. 'I like it. What made me think I knew anything about furnishing? I should have left it to you and your aunt to furnish the club.'

She shrugged. His interest gave her an excuse to behave normally.

'That would have been impossible,' she told him. 'A lot of this is secondhand. And some of it I even had to dig for.

'These horsebrasses—' she picked one off the oak surround of the inglenook fireplace. 'I found these rotting in a part of the stables and polished them up.'

He took it from her, enabling himself of the opportunity to touch her hand.

She drew quickly away. 'I'll show you your room. I ought to get back in case I'm needed.'

He was aware of her coldness towards him.

'No. You can stay and make me some coffee. The club can run very well without you for a short while.'

She made to protest before reminding herself that Chris was still her employer. He had ordered her to do something for him. And she would have to do it.

She breathed a resigned sigh.

'Very well. Your room is at the top of the stairs. It's the one with the double outlook.'

He took his holdall up the stairs while she

113

went into the kitchen. When he came down again she had brought a tray into the sitting room. He observed the contents.

'Only one cup?'

'Yes, for you,' she said.

He took the tray from her. 'Go back and get an extra cup. You can drink one with me. Then we'll both drive back to the club.'

She gave an irritated shrug. Chris was making things so difficult for her. But she did as she was asked.

When she returned she found him examining the Christmas cards she had arranged earlier on side tables. He had his back to her.

As he turned she saw he was holding the card she had received from Gareth.

'How nice!' he exclaimed. 'You seem to be getting on extremely well with the locals.'

She looked away, placing the cup on the tray and pouring coffee.

'Yes—that's from Gareth Hunt. He's a good friend of mine. He's the person who was so helpful in providing horses for the club.'

Chris's smile turned sardonic.

'And what else does he provide—eh?'

Stephanie met his eyes. Chris seemed to be behaving oddly.

She had hardly had time to glance at Gareth's card when she'd taken it out of the envelope that morning. Placing it mechanically on the table, she had set out through the

114

driving rain to the hotel.

'I'm not sure what you mean.'

He was quick to tell her.

'Evidently you haven't read it properly. Would you like *me* to?' He read the unseen message on the card aloud. ' *"Stephanie— nothing changes. It only increases. I live on in hope—Gareth."* '

She felt the colour creep into her cheeks.

Chris watched her with a hint of malevolence.

'You haven't answered my question. I asked what else this Gareth provided. I hardly think it's fodder for the horses. If it is I wonder why he hasn't put it on my account.'

She felt a burst of anger towards him. He was questioning an innocent friendship when all the world was publishing his new affair with the wealthy Frenchwoman.

'What I do in my free time is my own business. You can think what you like about our relationship. And now, if you don't mind, I think I'll return to the hotel.'

He made one last attempt to make amends before she left the room, calling her name.

'Stephanie . . . !'

She turned and he saw the reproach in her eyes.

'Never mind!' He threw her a bunch of keys. 'Take my car. Don't walk. I'll be up later.'

She accepted the keys, leaving the lodge quickly.

It was easier for her to keep out of his way for most of the evening. She glimpsed him several times with the attractive Frenchwoman. Yvonne Roget seemed to make a point of letting most of the guests see how well they got on together.

Later in the evening the older woman caught her as she was leaving one of the sitting rooms.

'Stephanie, my dear—I wonder if you will have a drink with me. I think we should have a chance to get to know each other. I am sure you must have read about certain things in the press. It is as well that I find out how our amalgamation will be taken by the members of Chris's staff.'

Yvonne guided her into the bar. They sat at a corner table. Stephanie summoned a waiter who brought them drinks.

She felt an acute embarrassment as the Frenchwoman looked at her shrewdly. It was as though the other woman was aware of her feelings for her employer. Stephanie fought to hide her dislike of her.

Yvonne Roget went on in her attractive accent.

'There—this is nice and cosy. Now we can chat in peace. Tell me how long have you been in Chris Denning's employ?'

'Not long,' Stephanie told her. 'About six months, that's all.'

The Frenchwoman raised her eyebrows.

'So short a time. Yet he has put you in charge

116

of his newest concern. Why should that be, I wonder?'

'My aunt is in charge, not me,' Stephanie said quietly. 'I'm merely her assistant.'

The other woman gave an understanding sigh.

'Oh, I see. Constance Reed is your aunt. Such a charming person. That makes things easier to grasp.'

Her eyes studied the younger woman closely before she asked her next question.

'And you, my dear—are you another of Chris's admirers? I fear that wicked man has left a trail of hearts scattered throughout my club in Paris. It is shameful the way he uses his personality.'

Stephanie felt herself shocked by her question. It was all she could do to keep her temper.

'If you mean have I had an affair with him, the answer's no, Madame Roget.'

The other woman studied her face.

'Then truly I find that remarkable. You must have a very strong will, Stephanie. I would have thought you were very much his type. I find it odd that he has left you alone.'

Stephanie hated the microscope the woman was putting her under. She hated, too, the fact that she had to pretend to be pleasant to this person.

'Perhaps Mr Denning doesn't use his charms on me because he knows I'd be impervious to them,' she told her bluntly. 'And I happen to look on my position in his concern as a job.

'And now, if you'll excuse me, Madame Roget, I really ought to be circulating amongst his guests. That's something that Mr Denning is always very firm about.'

The woman let her go. She had found out what she wanted to know in spite of the girl's denial.

It was clear to her that she was in love with him. And it was also clear that he was attracted to her, in spite of his rudeness.

She wondered what had happened between them. It was necessary to know if she was to put into action the rumours she had circulated.

She had considered from the moment she had met the good-looking Englishman that he would do very well as her third husband. They had so many interests in common. They were both wealthy. They were both astute business people.

Yvonne Roget did not allow romance to come into her thoughts. That was for lesser people. Any romance could be sought outside marriage if it was found necessary.

What she didn't want was for some silly little English girl to get in the way of her schemes.

She joined Chris again in one of the other rooms where she had left him. Stephanie was some way away, talking to a client.

'What an attractive young woman that is,' Yvonne told him carelessly.

Chris pretended disconcern. 'You mean Stephanie?'

'But of course. Such beautiful blonde hair. And such a perfect face and figure. You must be very proud of your find.'

He kept his expression guarded.

'I choose most of my women on those lines. She's not all that unusual.'

'Oh, I agree with you. But she has something extra. Maybe it's that air of a virgin. Perhaps that attracts the customers, too.'

He answered swiftly. 'I wouldn't know. Any rate, I'd have thought it unusual if she was. Few girls are virgins these days.'

Yvonne gave a laugh.

'Few of *your* girls, yes!'

He gave her a curious look.

'What are you trying to find out, Yvonne? Are you trying to find out how many women I've slept with? If you are, you're in for a big surprise. The answer is—far fewer than the gossips would have people believe. If I was to have had as many affairs as they credit me with, there would be little time to run my concerns. And, believe me, like yours—they wouldn't run smoothly unless I spent most of my time nursing them.'

She gave a seductive laugh. 'We are a pair of fakes, aren't we? We show the world a side of us that doesn't exist. We say—now, tear us to pieces. Paint us as you think the public would like to see us. We'll go along with you as long as it brings in the customers.'

He gave her a look of admiration. 'You, too? It takes one hoaxer to recognise another, doesn't it? Well—maybe it's good to drop the lie occasionally. It's pleasant to be just oneself.'

She put her hand on his. 'You may safely be yourself with me. Now, tell me, if you will, what are your true feelings towards Stephanie? I am rather interested to know.'

He balked. 'That has no bearing on this conversation.'

'Oh, but it has. We are being ourselves.'

'Not any more.' He shook his head. 'Come along—let's dance. There's not enough action on the floor.'

Stephanie observed them. The small orchestra was playing a romantic, Christmassy number. Chris was holding the Frenchwoman close to him. His lips were next to her cheek.

She felt a glow of jealousy that was difficult to disguise.

*   *   *

Chris arrived back at the lodge much later than her. It was about four when she heard him come in the front door. She had had little sleep and remained awake for the next few hours.

Rising early, she felt dull and dispirited. She decided that a ride before she went to the hotel might lift her enough to get her through another day.

The rain had eased. It was barely light when she reached the stables. Alison was already there. Stephanie gave her a smile.

'We really ought to pay you more,' she told her. 'You're always here at least a half an hour before time.'

The girl's glum expression didn't crack.

'I enjoy being with horses,' she said gruffly.

Stephanie invited the girl to ride with her.

'Come on—you take Sloopy. I'll take Swallow. We'll have a canter to the edge of the estate.'

The girl agreed reluctantly.

They left the stables, heading for the river, some distance away, that bounded the southern area.

Stephanie got off to survey it. It looked angry and swollen. The strong winds and rain had torn down trees from further away in the hills. She could see what looked like a dead sheep, entangled in a huge branch.

She turned away dismally. Winter had set in. Soon there would be snow. It was already blowing a blizzard in her heart. She looked round to see Alison studying her seriously.

'You go out a lot with Gareth, don't you?' she suddenly asked.

The question took Stephanie by surprise. She had thought the girl had got over her jealousy of her.

'Yes,' she replied. 'I enjoy his company as a friend.'

121

'Are you in love with him?' Alison asked abruptly.

Stephanie examined the other girl's expression. For a moment she felt an edge of anger towards her.

'No—I'm not. Is there anything else you'd like to know?'

'Yes,' the girl replied. 'Is he in love with you?'

Stephanie's answer was softer.

'He might think he is.'

'Has he told you so?'

'Not in so many words. But, then, I wouldn't dream of telling you, even if he had. You know, I really think you should patch up your quarrel with him. I think he's hurt because you always avoid him.'

'Has he said so?'

'No. But he talks about you a lot. He says you've been friends for years. It's a pity to let a friendship slide. Friends are more to be relied upon than lovers. You'll find that out one day.'

The girl studied her shrewdly.

'I can't understand why you're not in love with Gareth. He's easily the best-looking person in the district.'

Stephanie laughed. 'Looks aren't everything. I'd be fond of him if he was hook-nosed and hunch-backed. But my feelings don't stretch to anything else. I don't think they ever will.'

'Are you in love with someone else?' the girl suddenly asked.

The question made Stephanie come to her senses. She had allowed Alison to pump her about her relationship with Gareth. But her dislike still showed through. Stephanie wasn't prepared to open her heart to anyone about Chris.

She changed the subject.

'I think your cross-examination has gone far enough. Tell me—are you coming to the staff party this evening? It's for everyone who has anything to do with the country club. And that includes you—although you're only here part-time. You might find it rather fun. It gives everyone a chance to let their hair down.'

Alison had seen Stephanie's poster advertising it.

'I don't care much for parties,' she remarked.

Stephanie smiled. 'I suppose, since you once lived here, you consider a staff party beneath you.'

The girl tossed a strand of her auburn hair.

Stephanie went on. 'You might like to know that I got the idea from all the traditional parties that were held here years ago. Mr Grey, at the shop, told me there were some "grand dos" here in the old days when your ancestors used to have lots of staff. I thought it would be a nice idea to revive it.'

The girl's lofty expression didn't change.

'Gareth will be there,' Stephanie said softly, throwing out her bait. 'It would give you a

chance to make up your differences. After all—
it *is* Christmas. You don't want to carry your
feud into the new year.'

Alison rose to it.

'What time does the party begin?'

'At about eight. We'll be using the room at
the back that's now the smaller dinner dance
room. It was once the library, so I'm told.
Where the old parties were always held.'

'I'll think about it,' Alison said quietly.

Stephanie gave a smile. 'I'm glad. If you
want any help about what to wear you've only
to ask. I think long dresses would be a nice
idea—the more old-fashioned the better. If you
haven't anything, I've several spare dresses you
can choose from.'

There was no gratitude in Alison's green
eyes.

'Thanks. I'm not short of clothes—or
jewellery. I've got plenty of my mother's.'

Stephanie gave a sigh. Friendship with the
girl would never be easy.

Perhaps that evening she would be able to
show her that she had nothing to fear from her.
She knew Gareth was fond of her. It had shown
in his disappointment that she had never once
been back to his stables.

The rain began again, turning from a drizzle
to a steady downpour. They mounted their
horses, cantering back to the stables.

Stephanie left her and returned to the lodge.
There was no sound from either her aunt's

room or Chris's. She bathed and changed and went up to the hotel.

*   *   *

It wasn't until late in the afternoon that she ran into Chris. She met him along the corridor leading to the small dinner dance room. Her arms were full of greenery and Christmas decorations.

He stopped in front of her.

'You'd better let me help you with those,' he offered. 'Where do you want them?'

'In here,' she said breathlessly, stepping into the old library.

To her annoyance he stayed and helped her to arrange them. The other staff who had been helping had gone about their normal duties.

'We should have quite a good time,' he told her, as he wound holly and mistletoe over the central chandelier. 'I'm glad you revived this idea. I'm looking forward to it.'

She dropped the silver bell she was trying to hang.

'It's a staff party,' she told him firmly. 'Anyone else will be strictly but firmly directed to the other part of the hotel.'

'Yes. That's what I gathered. It'll be a good escape from the guests.'

'But . . .' Her irritation seemed to explode.

'Yes?'

They challenged each other silently.

125

'You're surely not trying to tell me I'm not one of the staff,' Chris said with a sardonic smile. 'As chairman of directors—advertising agent—staff interviewer—overseer of the Sunflower Club—not to mention a hundred and one other jobs for the concern, I claim my right to be here as much as you. As I said, I'm looking forward to it. By the way—who are you bringing as a partner?'

Her heart dropped. She gave a despairing sigh.

'I wouldn't have thought you'd want to be with the rest of us. I'm afraid your presence will have a restraining effect on the festivities.'

He clowned, especially for her benefit.

'I'll have you know I can be the life and soul of staff parties. I shall practise my knees up and the hokey cokey and dance with one of the undercooks. It'll be a never-to-be-forgotten evening for all of us.'

She said, with a dreary expression, 'I suppose you'll bring Madame Roget. I think it's incredibly selfish of you. I'd planned this one evening so that the staff could really let their hair down.'

'And I suppose you'll bring Gareth. And that will turn it into just another Hunt ball. Quite clever—that pun—don't you think?'

'He doesn't happen to be an outsider to the district. He's a local. And he knows most of the staff. Also he's not thinking about planning any merger with luxury hotels.'

126

'What kind of merger is he planning, then? By the words on his card I'd say he had high hopes of something. Perhaps a merger of *his* horses and *our* horses. Or maybe *you* and *him*?'

Stephanie glared at him.

'You're being facetious. I'm not in the mood for jokes. I didn't sleep well last night.'

'So I gathered,' he said with his grey eyes accusing. 'I saw you leave to go riding first thing this morning. It's a funny thing this love business. What do you and Gareth do? Make love on horseback? I should think that's a very risky thing to do.'

Her face grew furious.

'Why are you speaking to me this way? What have I done to make you so aggressive towards me?'

'I would have thought you'd know the answer to that.'

She looked back at him with sadness.

'It's because of that evening, isn't it? And the things I said?'

He studied her face. For a moment he allowed his heart to show in his eyes.

'You can believe that, Stephanie, if you like. Perhaps it's more understable to you. Yes—go on believing it—for my pride's sake.'

He dropped the streamer he was pinning and left the room hurriedly.

For a moment she followed his departure with her eyes.

Maybe she had been wrong about him.

127

Perhaps he felt something more for her than he did for any of the women in his trivial affairs. But, in that case, why had the papers publicised the rumours about a marriage with Madame Roget?

She refused to let her heart believe what it so badly wanted to.

CHAPTER TEN

It was a quarter to eight when Gareth knocked on the door of the lodge.

Stephanie opened it. She had just finished dressing. In her gown of off-white lace and satin that she had bought from a secondhand shop, she looked just as though she'd stepped off an old-fashioned Christmas card.

Gareth's admiring glance told her clearly what he thought of it.

'You look stunning,' he breathed.

'Thanks,' she smiled. 'I've only just managed to squeeze into it. We don't have waists this size nowadays.'

He eyed her slim figure. 'No one would guess you'd had any trouble.'

She let his compliment slide, telling him about her meeting with Alison that morning.

'I'm hoping she'll decide to come to the party. It'll give you both a chance to make up your differences.'

Gareth disguised any feelings he had for the other girl. He kept his tone light.

'The silly child. I never had any quarrel with her. It's she who's been cutting me.'

'You can hardly blame her,' said Stephanie, taking Alison's side. 'You used me shamelessly the first time we met. I can understand her being hurt.'

'It was necessary,' he said gruffly. 'She was making her feelings towards me apparent. I did it to stop her. She's only a child. There are nearly twelve years difference in our ages.'

'She's not a child,' Stephanie laughed. 'She's a young woman. And an extremely attractive one. I'm surprised you haven't noticed.'

'She's still Alison Noall,' Gareth said seriously. 'For years her ancestors were lords of the manor. You probably don't understand how important that is in this district.'

'I understand that you still believe we're living in the dark ages. Sir Humphrey lives in a modern house now. He's no different to anyone else. Anyway—Alison tells me her father was a tradesman.'

It was Gareth's turn to laugh.

'A tradesman—yes! But an extremely wealthy landowner as well, until his business failed and the properties had to be sold.' His expression grew sad. 'That was when he committed suicide. Soon after, Alison and her mother returned to the manor. Later, her mother disgraced the family. She ran off with a married man, leaving Alison behind.'

Stephanie's face fell. She had never heard Alison's full history before.

'Poor girl,' she murmured. 'I never realised she'd had such a bad time. No wonder she's sometimes sullen and moody. I wish I'd tried harder with her.'

Gareth shrugged. 'That's all as may be. Anyway—let's not spend the evening discussing Alison. Did you get my card?'

'Yes,' she nodded.

'And you understood the message?'

'I did. But you shouldn't have written it.'

'Why not? It's all true.'

She gazed at him, doubting it. Gareth's heart lay elsewhere. She'd suspected it for some while. Perhaps tonight she could be instrumental in bringing him and Alison closer together.

She glanced at the old-fashioned grandmother clock her aunt had purchased. It gave a welcoming appearance to the attractive hall.

'Come on. It's almost eight. I'm supposed to be there to welcome everyone with mince pies and hot punch!'

*　　　*　　　*

Only a skeleton staff, supervised by Constance, remained in the main part of the club.

As Stephanie opened the door of the old

130

library and switched on the lights, Gareth looked around with surprise.

'This is a do!' he murmured. 'You've managed to disguise the fact that it's a part of the hotel very nicely. Who helped you to put the mistletoe on that central chandelier?'

She looked up sharply. 'I expect that was Chris Denning's work.'

He gave her a sharp glance.

'I wouldn't have thought he was the type to take much interest in a staff party.'

A voice behind him told him crisply, 'Then you thought wrong.'

Gareth turned abruptly.

Chris's tone didn't relax. 'Perhaps you'd introduce us, Stephanie. I've an idea this is our horsey neighbour, Mr Hunt. Am I right?' He put out a hand. 'I believe it's you I have to thank for the prompt delivery of hacks. That was extremely good of you. No sooner requested than delivered from what I understand. I wish it was possible to say that about all the business I do. One has invariably to wait for everything they require in life.'

Stephanie introduced them. She was aware of their dislike for each other from the start.

But there was no time to dwell on it. As the staff began to arrive, having gone to town over their dress for the occasion, she welcomed each one effusively, taking over the role of an old-fashioned housekeeper.

Later, when she was free, she turned to see

no sign of Chris.

Gareth helped her to dole out the preliminary glasses of hot punch that had been brought to the groaning table. One of the hostesses organised music for dancing.

Stephanie stood back as people took to the floor.

Gareth began to talk about her employer.

'Something gives me the impression that he didn't take to me. I wonder why that was?'

She gave a shrug. 'He's like that to me most of the time.'

'And yet you stay with him?'

'Why not?' she asked colouring. 'I doubt if he'll be here long. You must have read all the rumours in the paper. It's possible he'll marry Madame Roget and set up his base in her club in Paris.'

Gareth studied her heightened colour. He'd already been aware of the look of admiration Chris had given her. Something told him the rumours about his marriage to the Frenchwoman were without substance.

He became even more sure when Chris returned to the dance and singled Stephanie out.

He threw Gareth an insolent smile.

'Since you're not using your partner, may I borrow her?'

He swung Stephanie away in his arms before the other man or she had a chance to protest.

The rest of the dancers on the floor drew

back. Stephanie felt embarrassed. Chris was doing his best to put a damper on everything she'd done. The staff were not used to mixing with him on an equal basis.

He had gone to the bother of dressing to compliment her gown. In his tails and white bow tie he looked slightly ridiculous.

One of the hostesses changed the record on the turn-table to an old-fashioned waltz. Chris took it in the right spirit and whirled her around until the lace on her gown billowed out.

He received the staff's applause with a bow. It broke the ice and they all returned to the floor. When the small space was full, he led her dexterously towards a window seat at the other end of the room where the lights were dimmer.

Pulling her down beside him, he pointed to his handiwork.

'Well, that's broken the ice. I don't think anyone will object to me being here now, do you?'

She regained her breath without bothering to reply. A wall of dancers separated her from Gareth. She waited silently for the music to come to an end.

'I find your friend a trifle stick-in-the-mud,' Chris remarked confidentially. 'I really think he should have tried to get the party moving like me. It would have been a good excuse for him to hold you in his arms.'

'There was no need,' she protested, 'until *you* came in. I told you your presence here

133

would restrain people.'

He drew her attention to the floor again. 'Then how wrong you were. Look—not one person is paying the slightest heed to me.'

She chose not to argue with him, but waited her chance to leave him as soon as the music ended.

Before that happened the door close to them opened.

Yvonne Roget stood there. She was looking radiant in a full length gown of scarlet satin. She had evidently paid full attention to the wording on the poster Stephanie had pinned up, asking women staff to wear old-fashioned dresses where possible.

The white rose at her neck line delicately accentuated its lowness. She had gone to a lot of trouble to leave as much of her bosom bare as possible.

When she saw them together she bore down on them with a small glance of recognition at Stephanie.

'So this is where you've escaped to, my friends. Stephanie, ma chère—that dress is enchanting. Where did you buy it? It makes you look so pure and virginal. Don't you think so, Chris? In spite of what you said about her.'

Stephanie felt her cheeks burn.

Yvonne went on gushingly. 'I had been asking myself where this wonderful music was coming from. And then I was told it was a staff party. So I thought—my dear Yvonne—you have every right to be there, since you are almost a part of the concern. So—here I am.'

Chris glared at her. He had deliberately disguised his mission when he'd seen her earlier. She was beginning to become a nuisance. He had merely asked her to the country club in order to impress her with the fact that his concerns were equally as luxurious as hers. But they had discussed very little in the way of business since being there. Yvonne had made clear to him her intentions in other directions. He was still trying to get out of the situation without hurting her feelings too badly.

'Quite!' he said tightly. 'So here you are. Isn't that wonderful? I'm sorry we didn't invite you. Evidently it was considered not quite your scene.'

'Oh, but I love staff parties!' she exclaimed. 'I think it gives all concerned the chance to become one big happy family. It is good to meet on an equal footing once a year.'

Stephanie was racking her brains to think of what Chris could possibly have said about her. Had he given Madame Roget the impression that they'd had an affair?

She felt her fury against both of them grow.

Smiling sweetly to cover it, she handed the Frenchwoman a plate of petit fours.

'In that case, Madame—since tonight we're on an equal footing, perhaps you wouldn't mind handing these around to everyone.'

While the Frenchwoman was recovering from her surprise, Stephanie handed Chris a tray of glasses of wine.

'And maybe, Mr Denning—you would do the same.'

Disappearing amongst the staff she made her way back to Gareth. She was just in time to see Alison entering through the other door.

The girl looked so different from every other time Stephanie had seen her. She was wearing a chiffon dress of pale green. It was full and complimented her tall figure as well as her tawny hair.

It was clear to Stephanie that the girl had taken infinite pains with her appearance. She found herself praying that at last Gareth would have his eyes opened. His reasons for not acknowledging he was in love with Alison were ridiculous.

As she went forward to greet her, a touch of selfishness made her wonder why she was doing so much for the pair of them. After Chris left, without Gareth for company, life was going to be very lonely.

But she didn't allow what she thought to show in her voice.

'Alison—you look gorgeous. Come and make up your differences with Gareth. I'm so glad you could come. We're all having a marvellous time.'

Alison came forward slowly. It was clear to see that Gareth was impressed with what he

136

saw. But he kept his greeting for her muted.

It took all Stephanie's persuasion to make them dance together later. When she at last arranged it, she drifted to another part of the room, weary of everything she'd tried to do.

A voice close to her said—'Ah, caught you!'

Chris's hand came out, capturing her own.

'You thought you'd managed to get rid of me very nicely, didn't you? Well, I've had enough of playing waiter. You can get your boyfriend to take his turn.' Chris's smile was playful. 'I intend to punish you,' he went on. 'Someone's put on a nice smoochy number. It happens to be right up my street. You can dance with me again.'

He drew her on to the crowded floor. The number of people in the room made it a cramped affair.

He held her tightly against him. The experience weakened Stephanie's resistance. She seemed to catch his heartbeats. They matched her own. For a while she allowed herself the unexpected delight of feeling him close.

His lips touched her ear. He whispered softly.

'Just imagine I'm Gareth—if you can't bear dancing with me. I'll pretend you're exactly who you are. I'll even fool myself that you don't detest me quite as much as you do. In fact, I'll imagine that you even like me.' He gave a sigh. 'I'm finding those very pleasant thoughts.'

He released her for a moment, looking into her eyes.

'How about you? Are you getting on nicely with your pleasant thoughts about Gareth?'

She started to escape and he drew her closely to him again.

'Just what did you say to Madame Roget?' she whispered fiercely. 'Did you intimate that I was another of your affairs?'

He gave an amused laugh. 'Yvonne tends to twist everything to suit her purpose. I'm quite aware she's been spreading most of the rumours the papers print. I'm having second thoughts about our merger—both of them. When I marry it will be entirely for love.'

He had steered her to a point on the crowded floor beneath the large chandelier where he had placed the mistletoe.

He looked up at it with a smile.

'I can't think why so few people have noticed that. Anyway—I now intend to repay you in festive fashion for the gross over payment I received from you a month ago.'

He captured her lips as the music came to an end. The dancers drifted away from the floor, leaving them together.

For a blissful few moments Stephanie let herself sink into his embrace, unaware of anything until the cries of derision sounded.

Suddenly she struggled free, her face turning fiery at the looks she was receiving.

In order to recover from confusion and

embarrassment she fled from the room.

Gareth went over to Chris as soon as the laughter had died down. His tone was scornful.

'Why did you have to do that? Isn't it possible for you to leave any woman alone?'

Chris retorted aggressively. 'What the hell are you getting flustered about? You and anyone could have done that any time you wanted.' He pointed to the mistletoe. 'Doesn't that mean anything to anyone any more? It's a poor Christmas when no one is allowed to take advantage of old traditions.'

Gareth's tone was still bitter. 'I'm not sure of your motives. But you've made a fool of Stephanie. I'd better go and see where she is.'

He disappeared from the room.

For a while Chris remained at the party. He tried to make friends with the attractive redhead Gareth had left behind, hoping that Stephanie might return so that he could in some way apologise to her.

When there seemed no sign of her doing that, he left to see if he could find her.

Madame Roget had been making her way over to Alison and Chris just before he disappeared. She stopped at the girl's side.

'What a pretty display of feelings that was,' she said, referring to the short quarrel between the two men that was now forgotten by the rest of the staff. 'It doesn't seem fair, does it, ma chère, two men haggling over the same girl?'

Alison looked back at her. The

Frenchwoman hadn't spoken to her before. But she knew who she was. She had seen her photograph with Chris Denning in the newspaper.

'Come and keep me company,' Madame Roget urged her. 'We will sit together and drown our sorrows.'

Alison went with her reluctantly. She had already had several drinks and didn't really want any more. But she was unhappy about leaving until Gareth returned. He had promised to give her a lift home.

'And what is your job here?' Madame Roget asked, when she had poured more wine for them both. 'Are you a hostess? Do you like working for Mr Denning? If you wanted a change I could always find you something working for me.'

'I'm not really part of the concern,' Alison told her gruffly. 'My grandfather used to own this place. It was our home. Now I help with the stable.'

Yvonne gave a laugh. 'Oh, I was wrong about you. Forgive me. But I am correct about you being in love with the very handsome dark-haired man who has gone out to comfort Stephanie, aren't I?'

Alison swallowed her drink quickly.

'I really ought to be getting home.' She stood up a trifle unsteadily.

'Oh, no! Stay with me. It is still so early.'

She persuaded Alison to sit down again.

'Please tell me what you know about this Stephanie. I find her a very fascinating person. There is something familiar about her that keeps making me think I have met her somewhere before. I have been racking my brains to try to remember where that was.'

The tawny-haired girl considered before saying anything. Some weeks ago she had unearthed an old newspaper. It had told her without doubt who Stephanie really was. She had saved up the information, wondering if she could make use of it. Jealousy, that Gareth still seemed to prefer the blonde woman to her, made her tell what she knew to Madame Roget now.

'You've probably seen her face in the newspapers. Her name's not really Stephanie Reed—it's Stephanie Hartland. She was mixed up in a police case in North Africa.'

Yvonne Roget drew in her breath.

'Ah—mon Dieu—you are quite right. Why did I not remember that myself? The news, too, was in the Paris newspapers. They made an affair of it. A crime of passion, it was called. But then the case was suddenly closed, as I recall. The woman was allowed to go free.'

Alison poured herself another drink.

'It was reported differently in England. Apparently an Arab tried to rape her. Later he committed suicide.'

Yvonne gave her a sly smile.

'Oh, you surely don't believe that, do you?

Since the woman was English it is only natural that your newspapers would report it that way.'

Alison stared at her. She wasn't sure why the woman had singled her out to talk to. But it was evident she disliked Stephanie as much as *she* did.

She listened while the woman went on. Some of it, to her fuddled mind, seemed to make sense.

'In France, crimes of passion have long been common-place. It was evident to me what took place. The girl had an affair with a good-looking, intelligent Arab. She had taken him away from his girl friend. When the affair went sour, she lured him to the cliff and pushed him over.' She studied Alison's face. 'Don't you think that is more to be believed that what you have read?'

Alison closed her eyes. The woman's face was becoming blurred. She wished she could block out the words she was saying, too. But they fell insidiously, making everything fit curiously into place.

'I believe that woman to be quite unscrupulous in her dealings with men. Clearly, she has set her cap at winning Chris Denning. So, I wonder what she will do with the dark-haired man now she is tiring of him. I do hope that she will not try to repeat what she did to the Arab. But, I'm sure she will not. Your British justice would see that she wasn't freed so easily . . .'

Alison felt sick and dizzy. She excused herself, leaving the room.

Yvonne Roget stared after her. She gave a smile. It wasn't often she gave vent to playacting. But the party had turned into a bore. It had amused her for a while to talk all that nonsense to that silly child who had clearly drunk more than was good for her.

CHAPTER ELEVEN

Stephanie, when she had left the room, had fled straight to the nearest ladies' room. For a while she had remained in one of the cubicles, weeping over the laughing stock Chris had made of her.

Then she had bathed her eyes and repaired her make-up, trying to tell herself that she was making a mountain out of a molehill. Chris had merely made use of an old tradition. She had made herself more of an idiot by flying from the room. If she had stayed, the incident would soon have been forgotten. As it was, she had only succeeded in making her feelings for him more apparent.

When Alison suddenly entered the room she attempted to smile.

'What a silly fuss I made about nothing . . .' she began.

The tawny-haired girl stared at her.

Stephanie went on. 'I'm glad you've managed to patch up your quarrel with Gareth. Is he taking you home?'

Alison continued to stare at her.

'What's wrong?' Stephanie asked. 'Do you feel all right?'

The other girl's words finally came out in a rush. They sounded slurred as though she'd had too much to drink.

'I know who you really are. You're not Stephanie Reed. You're Stephanie Hartland. I suppose you've been congratulating yourself that you've pulled the wool over everyone's eyes.'

Stephanie felt her face turn white.

'Who told you that?' she asked.

'Never mind,' Alison went on. 'What's more to the point is what are you planning for Gareth?'

'I don't know what you mean,' Stephanie gasped. 'But please tell me who told you my real name. Was it Mr Denning, by any chance?'

'Wouldn't you like to know?' Alison told her spitefully. 'Anyway—what do you intend to do about Gareth if you can't unload him on me? Will you do the same to him as you did to that Arab? Are you thinking of murdering him, too?'

Stephanie felt her senses reel. She took hold of a chair to steady herself. Alison was going on remorselessly.

'I'll see that you don't. I'll make sure that

144

everyone in the hotel knows you for what you are—an unconvicted murderess!'

She staggered out of the room, leaving Stephanie to stare after her.

Too shocked to burst into tears, she caught sight of her pale face in a mirror. Her lips moved silently.

Who'd told Alison about her? Could it possibly have been Chris?

Her heart refused to believe it. But who else could it have been? And why—oh, why if it *was* Chris had he done that?

No answers came. She left the room quickly. It was important that she caught up with Alison. It was imperative that she learned the truth. If Chris had been so unfeeling as to have told her who she really was, then she never wanted to see him again. She would leave the club at once. Anything she'd ever felt for him would be dead.

She went back to the party room, scanning it quickly to see if Alison was there. There was no sign of her so she went hurriedly to the reception area.

'Have you seen Alison Noall leave?' she asked Jenny.

'Yes. A few minutes ago,' she was told. 'She ran out without even wearing a coat. I nearly went after her. She looked quite odd.'

Stephanie stayed long enough to fetch her aunt's car keys from the office. Then she went out of the hotel.

145

The fierce, driving rain lashed the bottom of her gown as she crossed the courtyard. The estate car she and her aunt shared was in its usual position in front of the office window.

She got in, freeing her ankles from her restricting dress.

A minute or two later, she was driving along the road that separated the manor house from the lodge.

She caught Alison up just as the girl was turning out of the tall iron gates.

Stopping the car beside her, she wound down the window.

'Get in! I believe you're drunk,' she told her. 'And I'd like to know if Mr Denning told you my real name.'

The girl lurched towards her. Her long dress was muddy where she'd fallen. Her hair fell in dripping strands.

'Why are you following me?' she screamed. 'Why can't you leave me alone?'

'Get in!' Stephanie told her harshly. 'You're in no fit state to be out on your own. I'll drive you home.'

Alison had been gripping the window. Suddenly she went limp and fell to the ground.

Stephanie got out quickly. She heaved at the inert figure, trying to pull her to her feet. The girl struggled but lost balance again.

With a great effort, Stephanie got the back door open and pushed the girl on to the seat.

When she climbed behind the wheel again,

her limbs felt strained from the effort of coping with someone bigger than herself. She put the car into gear, forcing it forward through the wind and rain. Alison's sobs rang in the back.

Stephanie had passed the house where the girl lived on many occasions. It was the other side of the village, beyond the bridge. Although modern, it was of an expensive type and larger than the ordinary village houses.

As she neared the bridge her headlights lit up the swollen river. It was almost up the bank on both sides. Tonight's rain had added more than ever to the river's flow. She could see it swirling quickly and dangerously, lapping the highest part of the bank in many places, and threatening to flood the pasture.

Taking the car with care over the narrow bridge, she negotiated the bend and steep hill the other side. About fifty yards up the hill she stopped at the gates of Alison's house.

Switching off the car engine, she turned to the girl in the back.

'We're home, Alison,' she told her. 'Before I help you in will you please tell me what I asked you before? Was it Chris Denning who told you my real name?'

The girl heaved herself up.

'Why should I tell you anything?' she slurred. 'You've made my life a misery ever since you came here. You've stolen Gareth away. And now, like that Arab, you don't want him any more . . .'

147

'Shut up! And just answer my question. It's important.'

Alison was drunk. Her mind was hazy. But something whispered to her that if she told this woman a lie it would hurt her more than the other things she had said.

She opened the door, lurching out into the storm.

'Answer my question—please!' Stephanie begged her, getting out.

'Let go!' Alison shouted as the older woman opened the gate in order to help her up the short drive.

'All right—but just tell me who told you.'

'It was Chris Denning!' Alison began to laugh drunkenly. 'It was Chris Denning. Now—are you satisfied? You murderess! Murderess!'

Stephanie leaned against the bonnet of the car as Alison lurched her way up the drive. Her brain was in a whirl. Why had Chris confided in the girl? For what reason had he done such a cruel and heartless thing? Surely he must have known she would never keep such a piece of information to herself?

She hadn't even been aware that he knew the girl. But she was extremely attractive. Maybe he'd been trying to impress her. But for what reason? For what reason?

Stephanie got back in the car in a daze. Tears that had refused to come after the first shock now filled her eyes. She turned the car blindly, the soaking edge of her gown trapping itself round her ankles.

She allowed her car to coast down hill while she tried to free it. Tears distorted her vision as she approached the bend in the road at speed.

When she became aware of the danger, she fought to free her feet, slamming on the brake. Too late, she realised her mistake as the engine roared and her acceleration stayed the same. She had pressed the wrong pedal. But it was too late to make another adjustment.

Suddenly, and with a sickening feeling that nothing in life was important any more because she was on the very brink of death, she braced herself for what was to come.

Like an arrow, the car shot over the low parapet at the start of the bridge. As it hit the water it began to sink slowly into its murky depths.

CHAPTER TWELVE

When Chris found no trace of Stephanie in any part of the club he began to grow worried. Stopping in the foyer, he asked the receptionist if by any chance she'd left the building.

'She went out some while ago, Mr Denning,' she replied. 'I think she was looking for Alison Noall. The silly girl had gone out in the rain without a coat.'

Turning, he saw Gareth.

'You heard that,' he murmured. 'It appears she's got over her upset. Perhaps she'd enjoy the thought of our wild goose chase.'

Gareth's face had fallen. He realised that Alison had probably been deeply upset at him running after Stephanie.

He gave a sigh. 'In that case there's no point in me staying any longer.'

Chris watched him fetch his coat and leave. He began to blame himself deeply for the way the evening had turned out.

Fetching his car, he drove down to the lodge. He had no more stomach for the party. He decided to wait up until Stephanie returned and then lay all his cards on the table. During his search for her he had already made up his mind to ask her to marry him. He'd been aware of the way she'd returned his kiss. If she didn't feel something for him then he was going mad.

He waited by the window where he had a good view of the drive. When an hour passed and there had been no sign of Constance's white estate car, he began to grow restive. Maybe she'd broken down.

He decided to go after her. He knew where the Noalls lived.

Taking the road through the village he came to the river. He was surprised to see it lit up by the beams from police cars.

It looked ominously swollen. Men were standing on the banks. He thought they were probably worried about flooding.

150

He pulled up and got out.

'What's happened?' he shouted. 'Do you need any help?'

A policeman came towards him, clambering up the slope.

'No. We're all right, thanks, sir. But I wouldn't park there. We're expecting a truck. Someone's taken a header into the drink.'

Chris gave a gasp.

The beams shining on the water picked out something he'd missed before. It was the roof of a white estate car.

Dodging his way past the policeman, he clawed his way down the slope. Someone saw him and stopped in his way, preventing him from throwing himself into the fast flowing tide.

He fought his way out of the man's restraining hold, but others joined him, yanking him back.

'Oy! We don't want any heroics here!'

'Stephanie!' Chris found himself yelling. He sank to his knees sobbing.

*   *   *

It was a long time later when a police diver attached to a rope came out of the water.

Vaguely, Chris heard him telling others on the bank, 'No chance! The window's open. They probably got out but were swept down river. We'll probably find the body several

151

miles distant.'

Chris collapsed again.

He remained on the bank for much longer until the local constable, who knew him by sight, put a sympathetic hand on his shoulder.

'I wouldn't wait any longer, sir. You're drenched. And there doesn't seem much point. It'll be morning before we get the car up. If you like, I'll get someone to run you home.'

*   *   *

It was sometime in the night when a girl in a white dress woke up.

She gave a gasp. She was caught in weeds, lying half in a river and half out of it.

She opened her mouth and gave a fearful scream. But no sound came out. She choked, relieving her lungs of water. In a daze she dragged her body to the bank. There, she lost consciousness again.

In the latter part of the day she woke once more. Her eyes took in a watery sun. It seemed to fill the whole sky. She lay, looking at it. Her body felt frozen.

The sound of water filled her ears. She raised her head. There, in front was a river in full stream. For some reason the sight repelled her.

She dragged herself up, falling over and over again. Then she stumbled through bushes into a garden.

152

CHAPTER THIRTEEN

It was January, and the small church in the tiny village of Marshbank was full for the memorial service of Stephanie Hartland.

The mourners included most of the staff at the country club. In the front seats sat Constance and Chris Denning. Both were dressed heavily in black, as were the couple behind.

Alison Noall started to weep, adding her sobs to those of the woman in front. Gareth looked down at her.

'Would you like me to take you out?'

She shook her head.

'No, I must stay. It was me who caused this. I'm trying to let her know how sorry I am.'

Gareth put a comforting arm round her shoulder. The grief of Stephanie's death had somehow bound Alison and him closer together. The girl had suddenly grown up. He realised he'd been in love with her for years. Stephanie had been right when she'd tried to patch their quarrel. Perhaps it would please her now to know he'd come to his senses.

Chris sat white-faced, staring at the altar. Nothing much mattered in life any more. He had lost the one person who had meant everything to him. And he had let her go without her even realising.

A drear future spread out ahead of him. Not all the tears that lay in his heart would ever bring her back.

As the preacher's rolling accents told the congregation about her short life, he prayed that he could join her wherever she was.

When he left the church after the service, he looked around at the tombstones dotting the cemetery. They were partially covered with a thin layer of snow.

He found himself wishing that there was a place amongst them where she lay. It might have given him some comfort to have spent hours there, trying to tell her all she meant to him.

But there was none. Her body had never been recovered. There was a possibility that in time it would be found, probably when the river returned to its normal level. But that might not be till the spring. Perhaps it was better this way.

He looked up at the grey, snowladen sky. His eyes lighted on a white bird.

Maybe that was her. Perhaps she had come back to see how he'd taken her death. If it was, she would see how his heart was broken.

Oh, God! He began to walk with bent shoulders, resembling a man three times his age. What would he give to turn the clock back just one month? All his hotels—everything he owned.

But there was no bribing God. The brightest

treasure in the world he had lost.

*   *   *

Before another month had passed the village began to forget its tragedy. Gareth and Alison prepared for their marriage. Chris began to take an interest in life.

At thirty-one, the misery he had been through showed. His brown hair had begun to display a tinge of grey at the temples. It increased his looks, giving him maturity.

He had spent every day since Stephanie's accident at the lodge of the country club, trying to come to terms with his grief. Often he prayed for a miracle, that the river would give her back to him alive. But he was forced to see the folly of this.

One day Constance persuaded him that his misery might grow less if he returned to his London base and buried himself in work.

He agreed reluctantly.

'You're right, of course. I've no wish to throw a lot of people out of work because of my own selfishness.'

'I don't mean that,' she hurried on. 'I only meant that having something to occupy your mind might be some help.'

He gave her a weary smile. Constance, in spite of her own grief, had tried to bear him up. She'd been unaware of the extent of his love for her niece until he had told her. Then she'd said that she'd suspected once that he might have been interested in turning Stephanie into another of his affairs.

'I had very few,' he'd divulged. 'They were all in people's minds. You know how rumours start. Stephanie probably believed them like everyone else. Maybe that was the reason she seemed to despise me. I can't say I blame her.'

After Chris left for London, Constance threw all her efforts into her work at the club. The death of her niece hadn't lessened the bookings they were receiving. If anything, they'd increased them.

People who had read the story of Stephanie's unfortunate incident in North Africa were interested in seeing the spot where she had met her death. It grieved Constance to think how some people loved to read about other people's misfortunes.

*   *   *

At precisely the same time as Constance was thinking her bitter thoughts, a shaven headed man in a pantheon some distance away was doing the same.

The newspaper on his desk was one of the cheaper Sunday editions. It had grieved him to discover it on his premises earlier that day.

He was a kindly looking person in spite of his appearance. Dressed in a loosefitting tunic and trousers of a homespun material, he seemed to

156

have no shape.

Everyone in his sect was required to wear the same apparel. It helped to clear their minds of earthly, sexual thoughts, giving them time to dwell on higher subjects and spheres.

No one was permitted to live on his premises unless they adopted his own rigid way of life. His brotherhood was now thirty people strong. He found it satisfying to share his home with others of the same ilk.

He looked down at the paper again and his forehead developed a frown.

All but one, he mused. Whoever had brought in this newspaper from the outside world was clearly not of his ilk. They evidently still hankered for the corrupt world outside.

He picked it up delicately, hiding it out of sight under a pile of religious books.

He must find out who the culprit was. Already his mind was giving him a vague idea. Brother Leo must be asked to leave. He would allow nothing to contaminate the rest of the faithful.

He left his personal sanctuary, going towards a round room in the centre of the building.

Inside, a dozen or so people of both sexes were engaged in difficult yoga exercises. He gave them a smile. It was good for people to engage their minds and bodies simultaneously.

He stayed just long enough to ascertain that the man he was seeking wasn't amongst them. Then he climbed the stairs to Sister Nyadd's room.

As he'd suspected, the man was there. He was trying to engage the woman in conversation. It was a task that had preoccupied him since he'd found her.

Brother Samuel put up a crooked finger. The other man grew aware of him.

'Brother Leo—a word with you. Will you come to my sanctum, please?'

The younger man met his eyes.

'Sister Nyadd and I are engrossed in higher studies. Can it wait till later?'

Brother Samuel shook his head. 'I would prefer that you came with me, immediately.

The younger man smiled with watery blue eyes. He gave a sigh.

'Very well.'

He threw a small, backward look at the woman he was leaving as he followed the leader of the sect down the stairs.

Brother Leo wasn't entirely unaware of why he had been summoned. He suspected it was about his newspaper. He had purchased it when he had gone with Brother Yan to the local shop. It was his own stupid fault for having read it in the garden and left it on that bench.

But, so what? It would give him a chance to tell the silly old buffer what he thought about his secret sect. He had grown weary of the whole damn business. Actually, he'd been sadly disillusioned.

When he'd joined a couple of months ago, he'd thought the sect might be a cover for slightly more salty and earthly interests. He'd been waiting around for the fun to start. But apparently the whole thing was for real.

When the older man had sat down behind his desk, leaving Brother Leo to stand like a naughty schoolboy, he took the newspaper from beneath the books and held it up.

'Might I ask if this is yours?' he asked.

The younger man decided to dispense with subterfuge. The tone of his voice became insolent.

'Oh, thanks very much. I knew I'd mislaid it. Are you sure you've finished with it? If not I'll let you have it back when I've digested the more juicy bits. I'd been saving them till last.'

The man behind the desk looked at him with an expression of sadness. He shook his head.

'I suspected as much about you, but I wasn't sure. Whatever made you stay with us so long, Brother? You're not the first who's come here under a lie, expecting in his own tarnished way to find something more than prayer and fulfilment of the soul under our roof.'

Brother Leo gave a derisive laugh.

'Don't congratulate yourself. I didn't stay longer because I was weakening. It was only because of Sister Nyadd.'

The older man gave a sigh.

'Yes, of course. I suppose you've been trying to help her regain speech?'

159

Brother Leo laughed. 'God, no! I fancy her. She's a smasher. I bet you haven't noticed. I've been hoping she might take a fancy to me. But she's still in a little world of her own. I really don't think I can afford to waste any more time.'

Brother Samuel allowed his voice to become harsh.

'I agree you should not waste any more time. I shall be glad if you will pack your things and leave the pantheon immediately. And please, do not disturb Sister Nyadd before you go. Since she is already psychologically disturbed I wouldn't wish you to damage her mind further.'

The young man with the watery blue eyes laughed again.

'Tell the truth! She's off her noddle and you don't want me putting her in the family way. Well, you needn't worry. I'm not that hard up. I've never touched her, whatever you may think.

'Well, goodbye—and thanks for the pleasant stay. Oh—and my paper, if you please—' he picked it up from the desk. 'I'll read it in the train on my way home.'

With a slight flourish he started to leave the room. As he did so the head of the sect went to a prayer stool in the corner of the sanctuary. He deemed it as well that he rid his mind of anger as soon as possible. Anger was an earthly weakness. He must allow no abrasion of the mind to upset the pattern of his life.

Brother Leo kept his word about not seeing Sister Nyadd. He told himself he wasn't entirely a bastard. He had been extremely attracted to the young woman. From the moment he had found her wandering in the garden in her filthy, flowing dress of lace and satin he had fancied her.

But she hadn't been able to speak. She had looked at him in the oddest way possible, opening and closing those beautiful blue eyes of hers as though she was willing him to disappear.

But he hadn't. He'd taken her arm gently, using all the brotherly love he could muster, and had brought her into the pantheon.

From there, the leader and several of the Sisters had taken over. They had ministered to her. They had bathed her and put herbal dressings on her wounds.

Then they had dressed her in that hideous uniform of tunic and trousers. But even that hadn't taken away her attraction.

He had expected Brother Samuel to get in touch with the police. But he hadn't.

He'd asked Brother Yan about it. The man had replied in his oriental accent.

'When she has recovered her sanity she will be taken to the shore. She will receive kinder treatment here than in a mental hospital.'

It had seemed to make sense. Although he believed that Brother Samuel might have an ulterior motive. When all the other Brethren had flown out of boredom or disillusionment, he would still have one follower left who wouldn't question the pathetic faith he preached.

He tried to put all further thought of her out of his head as Brother Yan rowed him away from the small island.

Soon he would be back in civilization again. And he'd make up in no uncertain manner for his two months of celibacy.

Brother Leo gave a nod of thanks to the Chinese man as he climbed out of the dinghy.

'Many thanks. I've had a pleasant little holiday with you all. A bit boring at times. But, I suppose that's rather to be expected. Give my love to the others. Tell them not to bother to pray for me. I don't need prayers. Just a good old taste of sin again. It'll be like a breath of stale air. Cheerio!'

*   *   *

Once on the train Brother Leo realised with a pang that he'd forgotten to buy any reading matter for the long journey.

He uttered a prohibitive swear word under his breath, until he remembered the out-of-date newspaper. It would do to pass the time with until he reached Bristol and could purchase something else.

He took it out of his case.

Passing over the items he'd already seen, he opened the centre pages. And there his eyes rested on a photograph of Sister Nyadd.

His lips parted with a smile. It seemed he just couldn't get away from the girl.

He read the paragraph that accompanied the picture. A glint of understanding soon became apparent in his expression.

CHAPTER FOURTEEN

When Chris returned to London he spent several days in his flat before going in to the Sunflower Club. During the time he'd been at the lodge his work had piled up. He spent time going through the masses of paperwork his secretary had been unable to deal with.

Often he found his mind wandering. He relived the more pleasant times he had spent with Stephanie, placing them into niches so that he could take them out at will and savour them.

But the occupation grew unhealthy. At last, he forced himself back to the world of real life.

Hiding his feelings, he went back to the club one evening, uttering brief good evenings to the sympathetic staff.

Once in the main restaurant and cabaret

area he went straight to the bar. If he was to get through his first working evening there it would have to be with the help of several strong scotches.

He stood, with his second drink at his elbow, forcing himself back to his old gregariousness. He engaged the barman in conversation, asking how business had been in his absence.

A man at the end of the bar moved closer. Chris saw him out of the corner of his eye. He was a new client, slightly dissipated. As the man stopped beside him Chris saw his watery blue eyes had difficulty focussing. He was drunk, and accompanied by a colourful young woman whose profession was obvious.

The man began to engage him in conversation.

'Ah—is your name Chris Denning? I'd been wondering when I'd make your acquaintance.' He stuck out his hand. 'How do you do?'

Chris ignored him. He didn't approve of customers bringing prostitutes into his club. He wondered who'd given the man membership.

'Funny fellow!' The man gave a laugh, putting a shaky arm round his companion. 'I go out of my way to do him a good turn and that's how he treats me.'

Chris began to lose his temper.

'You've had too much to drink. Don't you think it's time you went home? The cabaret's about to begin. People don't want their entertainment spoilt.'

164

The drunk told him in no uncertain terms what he thought about the cabaret, using swear words to embellish it.

Chris gave a sign to a member of his staff who began to walk over. The drunk acknowledged it.

'Tell your bouncer to get lost. Did you get my note? The one I took the trouble to write? I left it with your doorman. I came back to see if the information was worth anything.'

'I received no note,' Chris told him. 'And I don't think any information you cared to give me would be of interest.'

He spoke a few words to the barman and the burly member of his staff.

'No more drinks for this gentleman. And if you get any trouble just see he's removed quietly.'

The manageress who had taken the place of Constance met him as he was making for his office above. She gave him a smile of welcome.

'Chris! I'm glad you managed to come in. There are several things I'd like to discuss.'

He gave her a small smile. 'Then we'd better do it in my room.'

He led the way into his office with the two way glass system. Once they'd sat down he listened to her rather trivial talk about the running of the club.

The everyday business that had once intrigued him now left him cold. He found his attention wandering. He began to play with a

165

letter that had been placed in the centre of his opulent desk.

The woman saw. She stopped her flow of conversation.

'Oh—someone gave that to the doorman a few days ago. He brought it up here. There was nothing to say it was urgent, so I left it till you came in. Do you recognise the writing? Would you like to read it before we talk?'

He examined it. It was handwritten.

'No. It can wait till later.'

He put it into his pocket, forgetting about it as soon as he'd done so. People often left notes with the doorman. They were usually asking for jobs. At the moment he had no vacancies.

The manageress went on with her business talk. He tried to commit his mind, making alternative suggestions to the already smooth flowing system. She seemed pleased.

Some time later she took her leave of him. At the door she turned.

She spoke with a trace of embarrassment.

'You realise, don't you, that everything you've built up—this club included—gives a lot of people a lot of pleasure? I don't mean just the customers. I mean the whole of the work staff. We might not be working if it wasn't for you.'

She stopped. What she was trying to say wasn't coming over in the right way. She began again.

'Constance Reed, who's an old friend, has told me just how much you've been through

166

lately. What I'm trying to tell you, on behalf of everyone at the Sunflower Club, is that we're glad you didn't pull out lock, stock and barrel. You treat us well. We might not receive the same consideration under somebody else.'

She closed the door behind her.

Tears came into Chris's eyes. He hadn't been able to weep since Stephanie's death. For a while he gave way to them.

As he pulled a handkerchief out of his pocket, the letter dropped on to the carpet.

He picked it up some time later and slowly slit open the envelope.

The note was brief and to the point.

'I know something that might interest you. It concerns the young woman in the enclosed cutting. I've reason to believe she's alive. Perhaps we could meet to discuss terms.'

At the bottom of the note was a telephone number. The cutting was still in the envelope. He drew it out. He saw a picture of Stephanie. The same photograph that had been used after the incident in North Africa had been used to report her accident.

He closed his eyes in a moment of intense anger, crumpling the letter and its contents and dropping them into a wastepaper basket.

When he opened his eyes, he saw through the two way mirror, the man who had accosted him in the bar. He had no doubt in his mind that he was the man who had written the note.

With rage bursting inside him he went down to confront him.

The man and his companion were preparing to leave. He was causing a disturbance, telling other guests what he thought of a club that refused to serve him with a drink.

Chris caught him up before he left, dragging him by the collar and twisting him round.

'Was it you who left me that letter about Stephanie?' he demanded dangerously.

The man gave a surly grin. 'Ah—you're interested. Then let's go somewhere and talk money.'

'Money!' Chris spat. Further words failed him. He felt he wanted to kill this person who feasted on people's tragedies and tried to use them for extortion.

The man with the watery blue eyes saw his disbelief.

'You think I'm fooling, don't you? Well, it's true. I know where the girl is. She was never drowned. I was with her a few days ago.'

Chris brought up his fist. 'If you're telling the truth where is she?'

The man laughed drunkenly. 'Heaven, dear boy! Heaven!'

Chris's fist slammed into his face. The man fell down heavily. He was about to strike him again when one of his staff pulled Chris off.

'I wouldn't do that, sir. Shall I take care of him for you?'

Chris drew back, his face contorted with

fury.

'Yes. Get him out of my sight!'

The drunk heaved himself off the ground. The blow had sobered him. Blood was streaming from his lip. He noticed Chris striding away.

'You bloody idiot!' he shouted after him. 'I meant the Brotherhood of Heaven. You'll find it on an island close to the Welsh border. If you want the girl—that's where she is.'

CHAPTER FIFTEEN

The man's words stayed in Chris's mind for several days. But he did nothing about them. He told himself the man was a drunken fraud. It would have been too much to bear if he had searched the Welsh border and found no such island. His agony of mind might have sent him insane.

Stephanie was dead. He had to face that. She would have stood no chance of survival in that fast flowing river. He had seen for himself the bodies of cattle and sheep that had been brought down from the hills after that night of storms and heavy rain.

He had to give up any false hope.

But, nevertheless, at the end of the week, he found himself still dwelling on that information. It began to haunt him as much as

169

her death.

Resigning himself he drove northwards. He must put his mind at rest, if only to prove that it was a lie.

He decided not to stay at the Minton Spiers Country Club. It would be wrong of him to raise Constance's hopes with the feeble story. Instead, he stayed at one of his hotels further north.

From there, he asked in villages around the country-side for information about the Brotherhood. He stayed in the vicinity for several days. No one knew of its whereabouts and he prepared to go back to London.

As he crossed the Welsh border along a lesser used road, he found himself following a river. In places it was wide, stretching several hundred feet across.

He stopped the car.

His mind told him that this was probably the same river that ran through Marshbank. It was vaguely possible that if Stephanie had managed to keep afloat on a log or a large tree branch after she'd escaped from the car she might have cheated death.

He dashed the thought away as soon as it came.

Why had he wasted his time coming back to this area where his heart had known such pain? She was dead. There was no island. He might just as well believe in fairy stories. The man had lied.

170

He put the car into gear and drove on. And it was then that he caught sight of the roof of a pagoda type building that looked as though it was on the opposite bank of the river. But the landscape opened up and he saw it was on a tiny island.

He felt himself break out in beads of perspiration.

*   *   *

Standing on the bank immediately opposite the island, Chris stared over at his find. A small, makeshift landing stage lay beside him. At a similar landing stage on the island he could see a dinghy tied up.

He began to shout, trying to attract the attention of whoever owned the house. But no one appeared through the bushes.

He went slowly back to his car.

The nearest village was a further two miles along the country road. It was dark now. As soon as he arrived he stopped at the small local.

Ordering a drink, he sat down at a table next to a middle-aged man who looked like a regular customer.

He offered to buy him a drink. The man accepted readily.

'That's good of you, sir. Yes, another beer would go down well.'

When Chris returned with it the man asked

him if he was staying in the village.

Chris shook his head. 'No. I'm looking for a group that calls itself the Brotherhood of Heaven.'

The man gave a laugh. 'You're not thinking of joining that funny bunch, are you, sir?'

Chris wondered whether he might be dreaming.

'Have you heard of it? Is it on that island I saw?'

The man took a mouthful of his beer before giving a nod.

'They're a fine bunch of weirdos. A shavenheaded lot. Out of *this* world, that's for certain.'

'Then you've actually seen them?'

'I've seen a couple. The rest stay strictly out of sight. I've got the village shop. Somebody comes once a week to pick up their food. Not the normal sort of stuff. I have to get in special things for them. Brown rice—cider vinegar—different kinds of vegetables and health foods.'

'How can I get across there? Can I hire a boat?'

The man shook his head.

'There's no boat in the village except theirs. And I wouldn't advise a call, sir. I don't think they take kindly to visitors.'

'Supposing I wanted to join them.'

The shopkeeper gave a loud laugh.

'You don't look that weird, sir.'

'But how would I?' Chris persisted.

172

The man's face straightened. 'Brother Yan's calling at the shop tomorrow. Why don't you ask him?'

Chris thanked him and left.

*   *   *

The following morning he was on the riverbank at the crack of dawn. For a long time he waited amongst the bushes until he saw a man leave the island in the dinghy and row towards the shore.

As the man reached the bank he came out.

'Good morning. Can you spare me a moment to talk? I'm interested in joining the Brotherhood. I'd like to meet the leader of your sect.'

The Chinese man was surprised to see him there. But his expression remained inscrutable. He spoke with an accent.

'I am afraid that cannot be arranged. We have no more room for initiates. I am sorry I can be of no further help.'

He picked up a shopping basket from the boat and set off along the road towards the village.

Chris watched him disappear. When he had made sure that he was not being watched from a distance, he got in and untied the dinghy.

He was unused to rowing and the tide was strong. He had to use all his strength to avoid being swept further downstream.

Some time later, he got out and tied up the boat on the island's landing stage.

Looking around he saw a narrow path leading through the thick bushes. It brought him out to a small garden in front of the unusually shaped house.

For a while he waited at the edge. Then he stepped out across the lawn. There were several stone benches. But none was occupied. He heard the noise of chanting coming from inside the house.

As he reached the archway that housed the entrance a short, shaven headed man stood barring his way. He was dressed in the same fashion as Brother Yan. But his face was less inscrutable. It showed alarm.

'Who are you? Please go away. No strangers can enter here. Go in peace.'

'I would like to see the leader of your sect.'

'That is impossible,' the man said. 'Brother Samuel is in meditation. All the brethren are in meditation. Please go away in peace.'

Chris had no intention of leaving until he'd accomplished his mission.

'I'm looking for someone who is missing—presumed dead. I won't leave until I'm satisfied she's not here. That shouldn't take long. Will you please fetch your leader?'

The man looked back at him uncertainly. The tall stranger had a determined look. If he turned nasty there might be a fight. He had better disturb Brother Samuel. Fighting was against his principles.

'Please wait here,' he said, closing the door.

Chris heard the sound of a lock turn. He waited several minutes before the door was opened again.

This time an older man stood on the threshold. His eyes had a gentle appearance. But they looked deeply into Chris's.

'Go away in peace, my friend. Whoever is with us is here at God's bidding. Be sensible and leave. But tell me first, have you molested our boatman?'

Chris grew angry. 'As yet I've molested no one.'

The man nodded. 'I am relieved to hear that.'

'But I shall change my tactics,' Chris warned him, 'unless you let me come in and examine each of your inmates.'

'That is impossible,' the man replied decisively. 'You will cause nothing but upset. We want nothing to do with the outside world.'

Chris pushed past him. But the man, though short in stature was extremely strong. He took hold of his arm, twisting it into a judo hold.

'Do as I say, my friend,' he said between his teeth. 'I have no wish to hurt you. But neither have I any wish to see my Brotherhood disrupted.'

Chris winced. The man released him.

Chris made as though he was about to leave, then shot past the man into the entrance hall.

Brother Samuel gave a shout.

'Brothers Nym and Omega! Stop that man!'

Two burly men in shapeless tunics that disguised their size rushed out of the central room. In order to escape them Chris tore up the staircase. He pushed open the first door he came to and stood with his back against it.

A moment later his attention was captured by a movement in the interior. He became aware that the room had an occupant. It was a woman with blonde hair. She came towards him with no glint of recognition in her large blue eyes.

Chris could only stand and gape. The woman so resembled Stephanie that he felt as though he was seeing her ghost.

Then the door seemed to cave in from behind him. He lost consciousness as he hit the floor.

CHAPTER SIXTEEN

The woman the Brethren called Sister Nyadd felt a slight awakening to her senses. The shock that had robbed her of speech and understanding received a violent jolt. It had been brought about by the sudden stimulus of noise in an otherwise peaceful building.

The awakening terrified her. She heard a whisper from far off telling her to lie down. She obeyed instinctively.

For several hours she seemed to dream, experiencing forgotten memories creeping back into her mind like phantoms.

She saw a road and a swollen river. There was a heavy ache in her heart.

All at once she felt herself flying into the air and heard a crash like heavy thunder. In darkness, deep and intense, she found her fingers clawing frantically, searching for the handle of a car window.

As she turned it, water rushed in, threatening to engulf her. It was all around—in her eyes—her mouth—her nose. Her lungs felt as though they were about to burst. She struggled with the strength of someone fighting a losing battle against death.

At last, on the point of unconsciousness, she became free of the constricting womb of the car. And now she was being carried by a swirling tide that seemed to drag her along with the strength of a man picking up a twig.

Her head bobbed up once and she found herself sucking in air. But it lasted only a second before the river pulled her down again. It seemed to play with her, bringing her close to drowning and then releasing her.

Suddenly she felt her body collide with a solid object. She reached up, clinging to it, pulling her head above water for the final time before blacking out.

The river gave up its battle, letting her go,

sweeping her along the waters of time.

*   *   *

When Chris came round he was being looked after by Brother Samuel in his sanctum. Some of the contents of his pockets were strewn on a nearby table. The man was examining them.

When the man realised his patient was conscious, he changed the herbal dressing he had placed on the wound at the back of Chris's head.

The action brought back what had happened. Chris sat up unsteadily.

'That woman in the room I was in . . .'

Brother Samuel cut him short.

'If you are sufficiently recovered I shall have you rowed across the river. I am sorry for the wound you received when my brothers broke in the door. But I am sure you will understand I was well within my rights to try to evict you. You have trespassed on my private property.'

'That woman—' Chris began again.

'You mean Sister Nyadd?'

'How did she get here?'

The man became evasive.

'She was sent to us by God. And now, Mr Denning, will you please leave us.'

Chris remained where he was.

'I was told by someone that a friend of mine—Stephanie Hartland, who was believed dead, was on this island.'

Brother Samuel gave a smile of understanding. 'I presume you met Brother Leo. I should discount anything he told you, Mr Denning. He is an unscrupulous man. His word is not to be trusted.'

'Then let me see your Sister Nyadd again before I go. If she's not my friend I'll soon know.'

'It will do you no good, Mr Denning. The woman can neither speak nor understand. But she is at peace with us. God has sent her into our safekeeping.'

Chris clambered off the couch. He went painfully to the door. But he had no intention of leaving until he had seen the woman again.

Brother Samuel gathered up his things.

'These are yours, Mr Denning. Forgive me for removing them. I wanted to satisfy myself that you were not a member of the press who might send others to disturb us.'

Chris took them from him. It gave him further moments to regain strength.

When the man opened the door of his sanctum, Chris saw the staircase ahead of him. He went to move towards it, but the man was faster than him. He barred his way.

'Please leave peacefully, Mr Denning.'

A sudden piercing scream from a room at the top of the stairs took them both by surprise.

Chris, in spite of his injury, was first up it. He bounded into the room he had been in once before.

The blonde haired woman in her shapeless garb was writhing on her couch.

'I shall drown!' she moaned. 'Oh, God—I shall drown!'

Chris recognised Stephanie's voice. He rushed to her side. Sobs of speechless joy filled his throat. He choked on them gathering the woman into his arms.

Brother Samuel, who had come into the room behind him, saw the man's emotion. He left them together for a moment, wondering what further action to take.

CHAPTER SEVENTEEN

In view of the fact that Sister Nyadd, in spite of her dazed state, seemed to recognise the man who had invaded his pantheon, Brother Samuel realised there was little he could do except release her into his care.

He had them both safely transported across the river.

Stephanie, who had done little but lapse into tears, let herself be driven away by Chris in his car.

He took her directly to the nearest hospital. There, for several days, she stayed in a state of bewilderment while psychiatrists and neurologists examined her at frequent intervals.

For a while she was allowed to receive no visitors. The specialists considered that a further shock, so soon after recovering understanding, might result in untold damage.

Chris resigned himself to wait until such time as he could safely see her.

That privilege was given to her aunt first. Chris forbade her to mention anything about the torment and pain he had been through believing her dead.

A few days later he was allowed to visit her himself. He called at the hospital expecting to find her in bed. But she was up and in the garden. Although still winter, a weak sun gave the day a feeling of spring.

A nurse brought him to the bench where Stephanie was sitting. She gave a small nod before leaving them alone together.

Words suddenly seemed to fail him. He found himself reverting to his old brusque attitude that he had often used when talking to her in the past to disguise his true feelings.

'Ah—you've finished your reclining, then. I hope you're feeling better.'

She looked back at him, finding herself growing embarrassed.

'I'm glad you came to see me,' she began. 'Constance told me it's you I have to thank for finding me. I remember little about how I got here. But she assured me you went to a lot of trouble.'

He gave a shrug, hiding his expression.

'It was nothing,' he told her. 'I'd have done it for any of my staff.'

A wall of silence came between them. Stephanie eventually broke it.

'Why did you tell Alison my real name?' she asked. 'It seemed a most unkind, cruel thing to do.'

Chris looked at her in astonishment.

'I don't know what you mean. I told Alison nothing. You must have an extremely poor opinion of me, Stephanie, if you think I'd do a thing like that.'

She gave a sigh. 'It doesn't matter. I still can't think properly. It's funny I should remember that. But I believe it was very important to me on that last night.'

He studied her, trying hard not to let her see he was at breaking point. He ached to tell her the pain he had suffered. But it was clear she wasn't ready for it. He had been warned not to alarm her in any way.

With an effort he kept his tone light, making conversation.

'You'd have enjoyed your memorial service. The vicar said a lot of nice things about you. Everyone sobbed and cried. It was really a memorable time. You'll have to thank him for all his trouble when you're out and about again.'

She looked down at her hands.

'Constance tells me Alison and Gareth are getting married. Is it true?'

182

'Yes,' he said quietly. 'I'm rather surprised she told you that. I believe you were fond of him. After the Christmas card he sent, it must seem hurtful to you that he found it so easy to fall in love with someone else so soon.'

Stephanie gave a small smile. 'I suppose it's only after we're dead people reveal their true feelings. It isn't often people come back from the grave, like me. Anyway—I tried my best to get them back together. Only it appeared Alison mistrusted me.' She frowned. 'I wonder who *did* tell Alison about me, if it wasn't you.'

Chris didn't reply. He had his own suspicions. The name of the woman he thought might be responsible came up in Stephanie's next breath.

'Have you completed your merger with Madame Roget and her concerns?' she asked. 'I meant to ask Constance but the nurse wouldn't let her stay long.'

'You shouldn't worry your head about my business,' he told her. 'When you're well I shall have you sent away for a long, carefree holiday. I don't think you ever really recovered from that business in North Africa. Coupled with the shock of nearly drowning it must have added to your illness.'

'I wouldn't dream of letting you do such a thing,' she replied quickly. 'I seem to spend my life in your debt.'

'Is that so very terrible?' he responded, forgetting the warning he'd been given. 'Don't you realise I've been handed a new lease of life? I owe that all to you.'

She looked at him without comprehension. He bowed his head, wishing he could rip out his tongue.

'I don't understand you,' she murmured.

'Forget it,' he said hastily.

She broke through another wall of silence, adding a further phrase to her previous question.

'Were the rumours right? Are you going to marry Yvonne Roget?'

He replied with amusement and disbelief.

'Marry Yvonne! Spare me that. I've cut all my connections with her. I found out that neither she nor her concerns are very worthwhile propositions.'

'But the papers seemed so certain,' she began.

He sighed, putting a hand to his forehead.

'You listen to too many rumours, Stephanie. You should know how people love to elaborate. I wish I'd put down every one that circulated about me and the many affairs I was supposed to have had. I've felt the way you've despised me on many occasions.'

'I've never despised you,' she said softly. 'I've only despised myself.'

He stared at her. 'Why do you say that?'

She began to cry softly. 'Since I'm alive when I should be dead, I don't suppose it matters if I make a fool of myself. I wanted you to kiss me

184

in the garden that night. And, when you did, I felt so ashamed. I had too much pride. I didn't want to be just another of your conquests.'

He listened in incredulous wonder.

'But didn't you realise,' he replied quickly, 'that nothing like that could have been further from my mind? I loved you then, as I love you now. I'd lay down my life for you. Later, when I thought you were in love with Gareth it made me insanely jealous. I wanted to kill him . . .'

He stopped suddenly. He was saying everything he'd promised himself he wouldn't say until she was well enough to hear it.

He caught her expression.

'You love me?' she murmured with a look of astonishment. 'You could really do that after the terrible things I said?'

Before he knew what he was doing he had taken her into his arms. He was telling her everything he'd ever wanted to tell her. And everything she had ached for so long to hear.

Their newfound existence bound them in a state of euphoria.

A nurse came out to tell the good-looking young man that the visiting hour was up. She saw them and gave a look of astonishment.

She was conscious that the girl had been through a very harrowing experience. Psychiatrists and neurologists had been discussing her case for lengthy periods. None of them could agree exactly how her treatment should be conducted. They had stressed that the girl was to take life quietly. But, just how quietly, had never been adequately defined.

The nurse was middle-aged and one of the old school. She had her own thoughts about convalescence. Warmth and love figured high on that list. The couple in front of her seemed to be giving each other plenty of that at this moment.

She slipped away quietly, pretending she hadn't seen them, leaving warmth and love to supply their own remedy.

We hope you have enjoyed this Large Print book. Other Chivers Press or G.K. Hall & Co. Large Print books are available at your library or directly from the publishers.

For more information about current and forthcoming titles, please call or write, without obligation, to:

Chivers Press Limited
Windsor Bridge Road
Bath BA2 3AX
England
Tel. (01225) 335336

OR

G.K. Hall & Co.
P.O. Box 159
Thorndike, Maine 04986
USA
Tel. (800) 223-2336

All our Large Print titles are designed for easy reading, and all our books are made to last.